GRACIE

GRACIE

A Novel by Suzanne Weyn

Screenplay by
Lisa Marie Peterson and Karen Janszen

Story by Andrew Shue & Ken Himmelman &
Davis Guggenheim

Afterword by Elisabeth Shue

Newmarket Press • New York

This book is published in the United States of America.

First Edition

ISBN: 978-1-55704-779-3

10 9 8 7 6 5 4 3 2 1

Library of Congress Cataloging-in-Publication Data available upon request.

QUANTITY PURCHASES
Companies, professional groups, clubs, and other organizations may qualify for special terms when ordering quantities of this title. For information or a catalog, write Special Sales Department, Newmarket Press, 18 East 48th Street, New York, NY 10017; call (212) 832-3575; fax (212) 832-3629; or e-mail info@newmarketpress.com.

www.newmarketpress.com

Manufactured in the United States of America.

Other Newmarket Medallion Editions for Young Readers
Akeelah and the Bee (ISBN: 978-1-55704-729-8)
Baree: The Story of a Wolf-Dog (ISBN: 978-1-55704-132-6)
The Bear (ISBN: 978-1-55704-131-9)
Finding Forrester (ISBN: 978-1-55704-479-2)
Fly Away Home (ISBN: 978-1-55704-489-1)
Kazan: Father of Baree (ISBN: 978-1-55704-225-5)
Two Brothers: The Tale of Kumal and Sangha (ISBN: 978-1-55704-632-1)

Contents

One

Sometimes I thought my older brother Johnny was the coolest guy I knew. He was smart and funny. Last year his soccer team, the Columbia High Cougars, voted him Most Valuable Player of 1977. This year he was captain of the team and president of his senior class.

And then there were other times when I thought he was just plain crazy. This was one of those times.

We were down at the town park. Johnny had given me a ride there after school. Both of us went to Columbia High. He met some guys for a pickup soccer game and I went inside the rec center to play Ping-Pong with Jena Walpen, my best friend since forever.

I beat her six times in a row before we quit. Jena's not exactly the athletic type, even when it comes to something as easy as Ping-Pong. She'd much rather hang out, have a soda, and rate the guys in our school for things like looks, humor, general hotness, and overall future boyfriend potential. That's what we did until she had to go home at four.

Since Johnny was my only way home, I was left waiting for him to finish the pickup soccer game. I went outside onto the field to watch. I found an out-of-the-way spot and leaned against a broken fencepost not far from where Johnny's old wreck of a car was parked on the grass at the edge of the field.

Off on the other side of the field, Kate Dorset, the head Cougar cheerleader, and her cheerleader friends watched the game, too. Once in a while they'd explode with cheers for a great play or dismal groans for a missed kick, just to be sure the guys didn't forget they were there. Those girls always appeared anywhere the boys were, and they especially liked Johnny and Kyle Rhodes, who were playing out on the field that day also.

Kyle was on the soccer team with Johnny and was almost as skillful a player. He wore his hair long like a rock star, and he knew the girls were crazy for him. He was so high on himself that I never wanted anyone to know that he had an effect on me, too. I didn't even want to admit it to myself. But the truth was, when he was out on the field playing soccer, I was always looking at him. Even when he wasn't doing much, my attention would just sort of drift over in his direction completely against my will, of course.

The soccer game ended and most of the guys left, except Johnny, Curt, Craig, and Kyle. They stayed behind on the field, still kicking the ball around and talking.

Then, for some reason, they all turned their attention toward me.

Instant freakout!

I was a mess! My long blonde hair was sticking out all over. I didn't even have on lip gloss. I was in torn jean shorts, a stained, sweaty T-shirt, and dirty old flip-flops. Of course, it was really only Kyle who I didn't want to notice me looking like such a slob. I didn't really care what the other guys thought.

"It's like hitting the side of a barn," Kyle said as they all walked toward me.

And then I understood what was going on. Instantly I felt like an idiot for thinking that they had been staring at me! They were interested in the half-empty soda bottle balanced on the fencepost. But what could be interesting about *that*?

"Come on, Johnny. We're late," I complained, just so I wouldn't appear totally awkward standing there doing nothing as they approached.

The four of them suddenly looked my way, as though up until that moment I had been completely invisible. I guess to them, I had been. But then I noticed that a mischievous light came into Johnny's eyes, as if I'd just given him a great idea. He juggled the soccer ball off his knee and instep as he turned to Kyle. "Let's sweeten the pot. We'll back it up to twenty yards, and I won't be the shooter. My sister will."

"What?" Kyle cried, disbelief, or maybe ridicule, in his voice. "Her?"

"Me?" I cried, confused. And then I realized that they were betting on which one of them could knock the bottle off the post with the soccer ball. And Johnny was betting *I* would be the one to do it!

Johnny held up a five-dollar bill to show he was for real. "Five dollars says it's so cake, even my sister can do it."

I played soccer with Johnny and my two younger brothers all the time. My family was so totally about the game, our last name should have been Soccer instead of Bowen.

My dad played in college and he was our coach. His focus was mostly on the boys, especially Johnny, who he said was "a natural." I was included in the games but not the training. Still, I was pretty good—for a girl, anyway. But I couldn't hit that bottle from twenty yards out. And I didn't want to look like a fool in front of everyone. "No way can I hit that," I objected.

"She says she can't do it," Kyle said, turning to Johnny.

Johnny came beside me. "I'll be right behind you," he whispered, hoping to convince me.

I lifted my right foot. "No, look: flip-flops," I said to the group, making it sound like an explanation, as though if I'd had on the right shoes, it would have been no problem.

Johnny just grinned. "So, take 'em off."

Kyle and his pals Craig and Curt stepped closer, suddenly looking more interested in the bet. I guess they figured they had just made an easy five dollars. "One shot, five bucks, and the chick's going to shoot barefoot?" Kyle checked, as if it were all too good to be true.

At that moment I actually couldn't remember what I found so fascinating about Kyle. It must have been something shallow like his good looks and his rock-star image, because right then he sure seemed like a jerk. *The chick?*

Johnny seemed to read my mind. "Her name is Gracie," he corrected Kyle.

Kyle had already turned his back. "You're on," he said starting to walk out twenty yards with Curt and Craig.

Johnny motioned for me to follow him out with the others. "It's your money," I muttered.

When we were about twenty yards from the bottle, Johnny set the ball down. Kyle and his pals punched one another, snickering. The cheerleaders had picked up on what was happening and were all watching intently, too.

Johnny knew that if I were going to do this, I would have to forget about all of them and focus. "See the target?" he said, talking softly at my shoulder. It was the same low, steady tone my dad used with the boys when he wanted them to get serious and concentrate.

I nodded, narrowing my eyes to try to block out everything else but the bottle.

"Don't look at the target," Johnny said.

I turned to him, confused.

"You want your eye on the ball," he explained, "ankle locked, toes pointing down."

"Toe points down. Got it," I confirmed.

"When you strike the ball, make solid contact with your instep," he went on. "Follow through to the target, head down…"

"Let her shoot already!" Kyle shouted, impatient with Johnny's coaching.

Johnny ignored him. "Keep your plant foot even with the ball, but the knee of your kicking foot…"

11

"It's too much to remember," I complained nervously. Someday Johnny was going to make a great soccer coach, but at the moment I was too anxious to take in all his instructions. With everyone watching, I couldn't hit that bottle wearing my best sneakers, let alone barefoot.

I shot him a look that I hoped would convey how desperate I was to get out of this, but his expression was unruffled and confident. "Wait till you're ready," he whispered. "You can do anything."

To wimp out—as I was longing to do—would have meant letting Johnny down, and there was no way I could do that. So there was no other choice but to get it over with.

I approached the soccer ball, looked at the bottle, and then away from it. My palms were sweating. I wiped them on my jeans and breathed deeply. Then I took two long steps back, waited a beat, and charged toward the ball.

When I kicked the ball, my foot stung like crazy and then the stinging zoomed up my leg to my knee.

I didn't care, though.

In the next second, that bottle exploded into the air.

Yes!

Kyle hooted in surprise. Even though he'd lost the bet, he nodded at me, impressed.

Johnny cheered, pumping the air with his fist.

It felt so good, but I was determined to stay cool. "Nice game," I teased, sauntering toward him. "What's it called?" Keeping up the act, I extended my hand for the five-dollar bill, which he surrendered.

Still smirking at Kyle, Craig, and Curt, I followed Johnny into the car. The motor was noisy and black fumes spit out from the tailpipe as we drove off, but I felt like we were leaving in a blaze of glory.

We were driving back home, both of us grinning our heads off. "Barefoot?" I said, punching him lightly on the arm. He knew I wasn't really mad, and his smile just got wider.

"There was never a doubt in my mind," he replied. Well, that made one of us. But even though I'd been scared and unsure of myself, it had been worth it—so worth it. Showing off in front of those guys who never believed a girl could kick like that had made me feel so great!

That was the magical thing about Johnny; he had a special way of always making me feel really good about myself. Maybe it was because he saw the best in me that I wanted to be the person he saw. It wasn't only me, either. People liked Johnny because they liked themselves better when he was around. At least that was my theory.

As he drove, Johnny's smile faded and he grabbed my wrist, checking the time on my watch. He cursed quietly under his breath and began driving faster. We'd be late getting home for soccer practice, and that would make my dad extremely unhappy.

Two

Johnny screeched into our driveway and we both shot from the car. Racing around the house, we practically slid into the backyard.

Peter, Johnny's best friend, was maneuvering a soccer ball through an uneven course of orange cones planted in the patchy so-called grass. I say "so-called" because whatever grass there had ever been in our yard had long ago been trampled into dirt by our family's perpetual soccer games and practices.

Our dad, still in the delivery uniform he had worn to work that day, was coaching him. "You're turning too late. Do it again," he instructed. Since Peter is on Johnny's team and he's always at our house, anyway, Dad long ago started including him in the daily practices.

Behind them, my two younger brothers—Mike, who's ten, and eight-year-old Daniel—were horsing around with a soccer ball inside the homemade soccer goal Dad had rigged up years ago. Jena calls the goal the Bowen Family Shrine to Soccer. Normally, Dad would be coaching them along with Peter and Johnny, but since we were late, the practice hadn't officially started.

At first, Dad pretended he hadn't noticed our arrival, but I knew he was aware of us. Dad didn't miss much. Ignoring us—Johnny, really—was his way of letting

Johnny know that if he couldn't be bothered to be on time, Dad couldn't be bothered with him. Dad wasn't real strict, except when it came to soccer. In his mind, either the boys were completely devoted to soccer and gave it everything they had, or they shouldn't even bother playing at all.

Who knew how long Dad would have kept up this fake ignoring business if Peter hadn't fumbled the ball when he noticed me? He did that a lot lately when I was around. Even though I thought of him as a sort of fourth brother, I'd begun to wonder if he had developed some sort of weird crush on me. I hoped not.

Dad finally spoke: "I turned down overtime. Peter and your brothers got here." Before Johnny could make an excuse, Dad kicked the ball to him. That was his way of saying that even though he was annoyed, nothing was more important than getting on with the practice. And besides, Dad never could stay mad at Johnny for long. Nobody could.

Johnny kicked the ball to Peter, and the two of them passed it back and forth expertly. I tried to jump in, but it was as though I weren't there.

"I'll be goalie," I volunteered, but Dad didn't seem to hear me.

"Mike! Daniel! Take goal," he told them. Instantly, they placed themselves in front of the goal.

"I could shag balls," I offered. But he was too engrossed in watching Johnny and Peter to pay attention to me.

I was still feeling so terrific about my amazing kick in the park that I was excited to show him what I could do. I wanted him to see how good I was.

While I stood on the side, watching, the guys began to play. Johnny scored and Dad's face lit up like a Christmas tree.

Peter retrieved the ball from inside the goal and threw it to Dad. When Dad stepped back to catch it, he finally noticed that I was there. "Your mom was calling you," he said.

I had been bursting to tell him about the great kick I'd made. I had decided to say that I wanted to play soccer, too—to be included in the serious practices, not just the for-fun games. But the dismissive tone in his voice made me so angry that the words choked up inside.

Go to your mother inside in the kitchen, little girl. That's where you belong. That's what he might as well have said. All the pride I felt over my victory at the park just curdled like spoiled milk. I picked up a ball lying off to the side and slammed it into the goal, making Mike and Daniel leap out of the way. The boys just stared at me as if I had gone crazy. They didn't get it at all!

So, while the *men* were outside running around, shouting and having fun training to become kings of soccer, I set the table.

Mom made spaghetti and meatballs, still dressed in the white uniform she wore each day to work as the school nurse at Columbia High. At first she tried to make conversation, speaking at top volume into the dining room from the kitchen. She soon realized what a foul mood I was in and gave up. What tipped her off? Could it have been the sound of plates slamming onto the table with a force just shy of shattering?

By suppertime I had pretty much cooled off. Dad wheeled Granddad in from his room on the first floor. He's lived with us ever since a stroke left him unable to talk or walk about a year ago.

Peter was eating with us, as he did about three times a week. Dad said he planned to send Peter's parents a food bill each month, but neither he nor Mom really minded.

And, like an eighth person at the table, there was a small wounded hawk in a cage. Johnny had brought him home the week before. He'd found him hopping around out on the soccer field at school and was caring for him until his wing mended.

"The paper says you're going to beat Kingston High," Mike said to Johnny and Peter as he scooped a huge ball of spaghetti into his bowl.

Mom brought in some soup for Granddad, and Dad began feeding it to him. "They're going to win States," Dad declared confidently, meaning the State Championships. "It's a done deal."

"Yeah," Mike scoffed sarcastically, "just like last year."

Dad, Johnny, and I scowled at Mike. Last year the Kingston High Gladiators and the Columbia High Cougars, our team, had been neck and neck for the championship, but the Gladiators clobbered the Cougars in the final game.

18

"They're animals!" Peter said, defending his team. "They're bigger, stronger, and—"

"It's the drive to win that matters," Dad said, cutting him off.

"But they've got The Giant," Mike reminded him. The Giant is what they called a kid named Albert McCann, Kingston's biggest, toughest player. He was well over 6 feet and must have weighed at least 200 pounds.

"He doesn't play soccer—he just knocks people down," Dad insisted.

"This is *our* year," Johnny assured everyone.

Mom had gone out to the kitchen to get more bread. "Let's talk about something else, please," she said as she came back in.

Dad leaned in and whispered loudly. "There *is* nothing else," he said, pretending it was a joke. Of course, it wasn't. To him, there really wasn't anything else. He went to pour Granddad some milk but the carton had only a drop left, so he went into the kitchen to get more. "What could be more interesting than soccer?" he said over his shoulder as he disappeared into the kitchen.

My family went to every one of Johnny's soccer games. We were all super into them, even Mom, who knew the game pretty well after all her years cheering for Dad and then Johnny. I'd watched closely at the final fiasco with Kingston last year, and I had some thoughts on how they could win this year. "We should play four-four-two and double-team that guy McCann," I offered.

"You read that on *what* cereal box?" Daniel asked. Lately sarcasm had become his favorite style of communication. It was incredibly annoying.

"Daniel!" Johnny scolded him for being such a little brat.

At that exact moment, the spaghetti bowl reached me, completely empty. Johnny snapped it up and shoved it at Daniel. "Fill this up for her, now!"

Daniel shook his head. "We played. She didn't."

Peter tried to be helpful by stabbing two of his meatballs and dropping them on my plate. I appreciated the thought but it was a little awkward, as though the meatballs were some kind of pathetic love offering.

"How cute," Daniel jeered at him. "Why is it you eat here every night? Is it because the food is so good? I don't think so."

Peter began to blush. Had he started eating here *every* night? I guess he had. Was it because of me?

"Do you even have your own house?" Mike taunted him.

"He just likes ours better," Daniel kept going, looking at me. He was getting to be a real little snot lately. I was about to smack him, but Dad came back from the kitchen with the milk and we always got into trouble if we hit one another at the table.

Peter took the opportunity to bolt before my brothers could embarrass him any further. "Thank you, Mrs. Bowen, for another great dinner," he said as he hurried past her.

"Oh, I washed that sweatshirt you left here," Mom remembered, and trailed Peter into the kitchen.

Dad noticed that the spaghetti bowl was empty. He and I were the only ones who hadn't gotten any yet. "Is there more spaghetti?" he called to Mom in the kitchen.

"Just what's out there," Mom called back.

Dad sighed and headed back into the kitchen to look for something else to eat. "She gets to pick from your meatballs," Johnny told Mike and Daniel.

They wouldn't disobey Johnny. Now it was my turn to make them squirm. "I'll take this," I said as I stabbed a meatball from Daniel's plate, "and a little more. I do so enjoy meatballs, don't you?"

I had intended to leave them each one meatball but Daniel gave me such an angry stare that I had to prove he couldn't intimidate me, so I took his last meatball. "I'll need that, too," I said with a smirk.

I thanked Johnny as he was feeding some of the Italian bread to his hawk. "That bird's never going to fly," Daniel said sulkily, angry about his lost meatballs.

Johnny turned on him sharply. "Tell him that and he never will," he said.

Three

After-supper cleanup was never a good time for me. I thought it was completely unfair that Mom and I cleared the table and washed the dishes simply because we were female. When I argued about it, Dad just said that he and the boys did other things, like raking and taking out the garbage. This argument didn't hold up with me because meal cleanup was a nightly event, and garbage was only twice weekly. Besides that, I helped with the raking, even though I didn't have to, mostly because it was fun to jump in the leaf piles afterward, though that was beside the point.

The thing, though, that bugged me the most about after-supper cleanup was that when the weather was decent, the guys went back outside and worked on their soccer some more. Dad had even rigged up big stadium-style lights so they could play after dark!

That's what they were doing while Mom and I washed and put away dishes. While I worked, I kept checking out the kitchen window to see what was happening. Dad was pacing back and forth as he talked to Johnny about what he should be doing on the field.

Johnny sat polishing the cleats of his soccer shoes, nodding. Mike and Daniel were there listening, gazing up adoringly at Dad as though he was giving them the secrets of the universe.

At supper, Dad talked as though he was completely confident about this year's big game between Kingston and Columbia, but I knew he was nervous about it. They had come so close last year, and they were close once again. He was determined that the Cougars were going to be State Champs this year.

"Johnny still polishing his cleats?" Mom asked as she handed me a plate to dry. I checked quickly outside and nodded. I hadn't even seen her glance out the window once. How did she know? "It's got to be almost an hour already," she added, handing me another plate.

"He does it for luck," I told her. That's what he had said to me.

Mom sighed and shook her head. "He does it because he's nervous; he can't lose." I thought she looked worried. "It's too much for one kid."

She was wrong. Johnny lived for soccer—like Dad said, he was a natural. He couldn't lose because it wasn't in him to lose.

Mom knew soccer and she liked it, but she didn't *get* it the way the rest of us did. It wasn't in her blood. Dad didn't think it was in my blood, either, but it was. It didn't matter that I was a girl. I'd learned along with the boys, watched all the practices, and even if I wasn't as good at it as they were—because I hadn't been allowed to train the way they had—I loved the game just as much.

*

The big Kingston/Columbia match finally came. That night our whole family crammed into the stands that were completely packed with spectators. Even Granddad was there, carried into the bleachers by Dad.

My friend Jena came, too, since we did everything together. Plus, though she wasn't particularly big on soccer, everyone in school was psyched up for this game. Kingston was our biggest rival. Like everyone else, she wasn't going to miss the chance to see the Cougars beat them.

Down on the field, in the glare of the night lights, Kate Dorset was leading the cheerleading squad. Coach Colasanti, who had been the soccer coach at Columbia for as long as anyone could remember, was excitedly talking to the players, who were listening intently from the bench. Beside him Mr. Clark, the history teacher, who was also assistant Varsity coach and Junior Varsity coach, was writing things down.

I guessed Coach Colasanti was giving instructions for the second half. Johnny had played really well for the whole first half of the game, but some of the others hadn't done as well. Kyle missed a few passes. I knew because, as always, I had my eye on him, and there had been some other bad plays, as well. There was no score, but Kingston was threatening.

Peter looked up and saw me watching. He hadn't played at all; he was second-string and spent almost all his time warming the bench. I waved to him and he waved back, then turned away quickly.

The game began again. Almost instantly, a Kingston player stole the ball and began running toward our goal. "No! No! No! No!" I shouted.

Dad was on his feet, screaming!

Then the ball was flying through the air!

The Kingston crowd roared. "Kingston scores!" the announcer shouted.

I slumped in defeat. Jena seemed happy, though, as she breathed in something I didn't notice. "Smell that, Gracie," she said. "It's raw testosterone. You need high concentrations of the stuff to smell it, but there's more than enough here tonight. I may not love soccer, but I love to watch the players."

I nodded, thinking of Kyle.

Suddenly, though, I forgot all about Kyle.

Johnny was off with the ball, headed for Kingston's goal. I was on my feet alongside Dad, Mom, and the boys.

Johnny faked out the last defender and had a momentary opening. He took a hard shot at the sliding goalie and scored!

My family must have been cheering so loudly that we attracted attention. Some of the players looked up at us. One of them was Kyle. He winked at me.

Jena gasped. "Ohmygod, Gracie! He winked at you! Did you see it?"

I didn't know what to say, so I ignored her.

"Don't tell me you're not interested," she insisted, shoving me lightly. "He is so hot!"

"I'm interested," I admitted, dimly aware of the action that had resumed on the field.

Just then another roar erupted from the Kingston crowd. I shot my attention back to the field, eager to know what I'd missed.

The referee was blowing his whistle. The official time for the game had expired. With the score 1–1, the outcome had to be decided by a tiebreaker. Each team would take turns at penalty shots. The team with the most goals after five players shot would be the winner.

So the players from each team shot one after the other, going from team to team, four times. The suspense was intense. Each of the players scored.

Then the fifth Kingston player, The Giant, slammed it into the lower corner.

The Kingston crowd went wild.

He'd scored the go-ahead goal. It meant the Cougars had to score or the game was over.

Johnny was our best player so, naturally, he was the one to attempt the kick. The crowd around me grew completely silent as he stepped up to the ball and placed it twelve yards out from the goal. Mom and Dad held hands, barely breathing.

The ref blew his whistle to signal that it was time to shoot. Johnny took a few steps back.

"C'mon, Johnny!" Dad bellowed, his voice piercing the silence.

"Breathe," I whispered fervently to Johnny, hoping he could somehow sense how much I wanted this for him. Sure, I wanted the Cougars to win, but really, even more, I hoped my brother would be the one to win it. I knew how much it meant to him.

Crossing my fingers, I closed my eyes. "You can do anything," I said softly, trying to return the confidence he had given to me the other day.

Opening my eyes again, I saw his powerful strike. The ball flew toward the upper-left-hand corner of the net—and at the last second veered ever so slightly, slamming off the post!

My jaw dropped at the same time that Dad's head dropped and Mom sat down. Jena grabbed my hand sympathetically.

It took a moment for the Kingston crowd to realize they'd won, but when they did, they went wild with jubilant shouting and cheers.

The Kingston players jumped into one another's arms, and their spectators crowded onto the field. For a moment, I lost sight of Johnny and scanned the field eagerly to catch sight of him. Then I found him. He was crouched and alone, holding his head in his hands.

My family sat quietly, miserably, as the bleachers emptied out. Then Dad stood and lifted Granddad. Mom, Mike, and Daniel followed him. Together, they headed toward the car in silence. But I couldn't go with them. I had to find Johnny and make sure he was okay.

I said good-bye to Jena and went to wait in the field outside the boys' locker room. I hadn't worn my watch, but it felt like a long time before the first players began to leave. I nodded to Peter, who nodded back as he came out.

Kyle came out and gave me a kind of *look* meant to be sexy, I guess, but right then I couldn't pay attention to him. I needed to see Johnny. "He in there?" I asked. Kyle nodded, so I brushed past him and slipped inside.

Johnny was sitting in the locker room on a bench all alone, showered and dressed, but not moving. "Hey," I said softly, settling beside him.

He looked up but didn't reply.

"You scored a great goal," I commented, trying to be upbeat but knowing I wasn't really helping.

"Dad send you?" he asked miserably.

I shook my head. "No."

He just grunted. I wished so badly that I could roll back time, find a way to give him another shot at that ball. He didn't deserve this defeat. He'd played so well and given it all he had. This was not fair!

"Your team's waiting," I mentioned. Win or lose, the Cougars always went out for pizza after every game.

"I'm not going with them," he said. He sat straighter and pounded his knees. "It was supposed to go in! I put it right there! I blew it!"

I raised my index finger and pretended to be Dad, quoting one of his favorite expressions: "You know, son," I said in a deep voice, "you win as a team and you lose as a team and—"

"To hell with that!" Johnny interrupted bitterly.

"Know what?" I said. "You're right. You were terrible out there." I hoped some reverse psychology might work. I was getting desperate.

It made him crack a smile, at least. "Yeah, I was. Big time," he agreed. He reached for some wet towels and chucked them at me. I laughed and ducked away. He laughed, too.

"Come on, they're waiting," I said, smiling.

Johnny nodded and got up. We walked out of the locker room together. Not too far away, some of his teammates waited for him in a car. He waved bye to me as he got in with them. I waved back, happy that I had cheered him up a little.

*

My eyes opened in the middle of the night. At first I didn't understand why I had awakened, but then I heard people talking. *Was it Johnny Carson on his late-night talk show?* It seemed too loud for that.

Sitting up in the dark, I listened hard. Dad was talking to another man at the front door. *Why would someone come over at this hour of the night?*

I went out into the hall and looked down from the top of the stairs. Mom was there beside Dad now. They were talking to Sal Brown, a local policeman.

I could only hear pieces of what he was saying, but it was enough. "They were crossing Route 1...a drunk driver wouldn't yield...Johnny was thrown from the car...."

"Where's Johnny?" Mom demanded, already going for her purse. "Which hospital? I have to get there. Johnny needs me."

I saw Officer Brown look at Dad, and my heart seemed to stop.

"Johnny's at McCarthy's funeral home," Officer Brown said.

Mom clutched Dad, who staggered backward slightly. She sank to the floor, wailing as though her insides were being torn out.

But I just stood there at the top of the stairs blinking, bewildered. I didn't know why Officer Brown would say something like that.

There was no way Johnny could be dead. He was too alive to die.

Four

I didn't cry that night or even the next day. But the funeral finally made it real. Once the tears began, I cried until my face was a big swollen red thing with two slits for eyes, and then cried even more.

Johnny's death made a giant hole in the universe. The pain was unbearable; it made me curl up in a ball and wish I could float away, never to return. Johnny dying was so unbelievable, unimaginable, that it made everything else unreal.

When sorrow is as deep and awful as ours was, everyone shows it differently.

I didn't see Dad cry once, but after the funeral he attacked the goal in the backyard, ripping it down, tearing at the back sheets like a wounded animal.

Mom retreated inside herself, becoming very quiet. She hugged Mike, Daniel, and me a lot. She wanted to stay strong for us, but one time I went to the laundry room and found her weeping into one of Johnny's sweatshirts.

After about a week, Mom and Dad insisted that we go back to school. They would be going back to work, too. I didn't know how they could or how we would manage, but Monday morning we all got dressed and sat down to breakfast. "What if somebody asks something?" Daniel wanted to know.

"Tell the truth," Mom advised gently. "He died in a car accident."

"What if they want details?" Mike pressed.

"There are no details," she replied evenly.

Dad was feeding Granddad at the other end of the table. "He died instantly. He didn't see it coming. Dying doesn't hurt," he added firmly. That was what he had to believe and I had to believe it, too.

Glancing up from my eggs, I saw that Peter had come in from the kitchen. He just stood in the doorway, shifting uneasily from foot to foot.

"Peter, come in," Mom invited him warmly.

"Am I still giving rides to school?" he asked. It must have been tough for him to say those words because normally Johnny would have driven us. No doubt, Mom had asked him to come.

At that moment I knew I couldn't face it. "Do I have to go?" I asked pleadingly.

"Everyone goes today—and tonight," my father insisted. His tone left no room for argument—but he had to be kidding! Did he actually expect us to go to the soccer awards dinner that night? It would be complete torture!

I opened my mouth to argue with him, but Mom shot me a look that made me think better of it. It said: *Don't push him right now.*

With a rumbling sigh of discontent, I grabbed my books and slammed out the back door behind Peter, Mike, and Daniel.

*

School was as bad as I'd expected. Johnny's death had changed me in some way I couldn't understand. I only knew that I was different now. I no longer wanted to goof around in the hall or talk about what had been on TV the night before or complain about homework or the cafeteria food. It had all suddenly become so meaningless, so unimportant.

Jena knew I didn't feel much like talking and she just stayed with me, walking by my side in the hall, sitting quietly with me at lunch. I probably acted like I hardly noticed her, but I was glad she was there. It couldn't have been easy for her, since Jena was never one to be quiet for long.

Around suppertime, nobody but Dad wanted to go to the soccer awards dinner. He insisted that we all get ready, but we just poked around, moving in slow motion, even Mom—especially Mom. I didn't know why he was doing this to us. It would be like the funeral all over again.

We all dawdled around for so long that the dinner was nearly over by the time we arrived. Coach Colasanti was giving an award for the most improved player when we took our seats at an empty table.

Coach Colasanti caught Dad's eye, and I knew he was about to say something about Johnny. My stomach clenched. Did he have to? It was only right, I suppose, but I didn't know if I could sit through it.

"I couldn't close this evening without a few words for a boy who is not here," he began, and instantly a tingling came under my eyes. I bit my lip, determined not to cry. "A boy who was not only extraordinarily gifted," he went on, "but also the best damn team player and all-around human being I've ever had the honor of coaching. I'm talking about Johnny Bowen. In his honor, I am retiring the number seven. No one can, or ever will, fill Johnny's cleats."

Dad must have known this was happening. That's why he insisted we be there. The coach looked at him. "Bryan, want to come up here and say a few words?" he requested.

Everyone clapped respectfully as Dad went to the podium. "Thank you," Dad began. "This means a lot to my wife, Lindsay, to me, and our whole family." Dad paused, his eyes darting over the audience. I think he was deciding if he should say more or sit down.

"Johnny loved you guys," he continued after a moment. "He loved this game. He loved this place. More than anything, he wanted to beat Kingston and make our town proud."

When he talked about beating Kingston, his voice cracked with emotion. It probably hit him that Johnny's last memory of soccer had been one of defeat. I didn't want to be reminded of that, either, so I pushed the thought aside. I wanted Dad to sit down and not say any more.

He didn't sit, though. "He never saw that win," he said, his voice shaky. "But don't be sad for him. Just go out next season and beat Kingston! You can still do it! You can make his dream come true!"

Everyone in the room stood, applauding hard. You could tell how much they loved Johnny—not as much as we did, but still....

At that moment I was glad Dad had insisted we come to the dinner. Johnny would have wanted us here because the team meant everything to him. And I was being reminded how much he meant to the team. It was right that his family should be here to represent him.

I couldn't get this idea out of my head for the rest of the evening. We were the ones who had to stand up and remind everyone what Johnny meant. It was up to us to keep the memory alive of all Johnny had achieved. It was what Dad hoped a win against Kingston next season would do. I wanted to help Dad, but I didn't know how.

That night I was exhausted and fell asleep fast. In the middle of the night, though, my eyes opened and I couldn't get back to sleep. I still had Johnny on my mind. I had the feeling I'd been dreaming about him, although I couldn't recall the details.

Tossing back my covers, I slid out of bed, making my way to his room down the hall. It was still the way it had always looked, only neater, since Johnny wasn't living in it anymore.

I walked softly around the quiet moonlit room looking at Johnny's trophies, plaques, and team photos. There was a poster on the wall of his hero, the soccer player

Pelé. His wounded hawk sat on its perch in the cage, sleeping.

I sat on Johnny's bed, sensing him all around me. It was a good feeling. Johnny could still be my big brother, my friend and protector, as long as I kept in touch with his presence like this. I pulled his covers around me and felt like he was there telling me that everything would be all right.

Leaning over, I scooped up his soccer ball that lay on the floor by his desk and kissed it lightly. It was the same ball Johnny had set down for me to kick just a little while ago. I recalled that day, how good I'd felt that my brother had so much confidence in my ability. Even though Dad didn't think a girl could play soccer, Johnny knew what I could do.

In the morning I awoke with a gray wash of light in my eyes. I had fallen asleep in Johnny's bed.

While I slept, a plan must have formed in my head because in the morning I was absolutely sure about what I needed to do.

With Johnny's soccer ball tucked under my arm, I headed downstairs to share my plan with my family.

Five

"I have an announcement," I said, standing in the doorway, Johnny's soccer ball still under my arm. My family was all dressed and seated for breakfast. They looked up at me quizzically, their eyes alert with interest. "I know how we can beat Kingston next season," I told them.

There was no response other than their puzzled expressions.

"I'm going to play in Johnny's place," I stated. "Dad's going to train me."

Still no one said anything. They just sat there, stunned.

Figuring that it was a positive sign that they weren't objecting, I took my seat and poured myself a bowl of cereal. "We have nine months before team tryouts," I said, and I began to explain my plan for getting into good training shape.

Dad let out a blast of laughter.

Daniel and Mike followed his lead, snickering and giggling.

The only one not laughing was Mom; she just watched the whole scene, perplexed and unhappy.

I stared at them as anger welled up inside. Did they really think I was just going to sit there and let them try to humiliate me?

I wasn't the same girl I had been before Johnny's death. Back then, I'd let them cut me out of practices and ignore me during games. No more.

I couldn't look at their awful, laughing faces another second. Furious, I stormed from the table, tearing through the kitchen to the backyard. Icy rain was pouring down on me, but I didn't care. Nothing would make me go back inside that house.

Dad was right behind me, standing on the back stoop to stay dry. "Gracie, sweetheart, I'm sorry," he called through the pelting rain.

I wasn't ready to accept his apology. "You wouldn't laugh at Mike or Daniel," I insisted angrily.

"Because they're *boys*," he said, as though that were an explanation I should understand.

"You said at the banquet to go out and beat Kingston," I reminded him.

"I didn't mean you."

His words began to sink in. He didn't think I could compete—and he thought that for only one reason: because I was a girl.

I grabbed a muddy soccer ball from the dirt and placed it in front of the half-torn-down goal. Rain splashed in my eyes but I whisked it away. "Watch this!" I told Dad. "Top corner."

I kicked the ball, smashing it exactly into the top corner, just as I'd said I would. Turning to him, I stared at Dad defiantly. What could he say to *that?*

He left the stoop, rain soaking his uniform. "Good shot, but not good enough," he remarked.

"It was right in the upper corner!" I pointed out indignantly.

"With no goalkeeper, no one blocking; it had nothing on it," he shot back. "It was a meatball. Your Gran could have knocked it down with her handbag."

I turned away. He wasn't going to give me a break no matter what I did.

He kicked the ball up and bounced it into his hands. "Is Peter here yet?" he shouted into the kitchen doorway.

In a moment, Peter appeared, followed by Mike and Daniel. "Stand over there," Dad told Peter. "Daniel and Mike, go one-on-one to goal. Come on!"

Obediently, the boys stepped into the pouring rain. Peter looked wary, like he didn't quite understand what was happening and wasn't sure he wanted any part of it, but he did as Dad asked. Mom came out with her raincoat over her shoulders and watched from the stoop.

"Play for real. Don't go easy," I told them.

Dad tossed me the ball, and I dribbled it to the other side of the yard. The dirt and patchy grass were muddy, but I kept good control of the ball as I moved toward Peter. When I felt I was in a good position, I started to make my move to shoot, but Peter stole the ball away.

Mike and Daniel cheered for Peter, but Dad shut them up with a look. "Try it again," he told me.

41

Going back across the yard with the ball, I headed for the goal again. And again, Peter got the ball away from me at the last minute.

"Again," Dad said.

Okay, I saw what he was getting at. It only meant I had to change strategies. This time, I shot before Peter could get to me. But he jumped in front and it threw me off balance just a little as I kicked. The ball sailed wide of the goal.

"That's enough, Bryan," Mom called to Dad from the stoop.

He didn't pay attention to her as he picked up the ball. "Gracie, get around him. Do it again."

I had to get it this time. Everything I wanted to do depended on it. I took my time setting up, just as Johnny always told me to. Then I charged at Peter, hoping the sheer force of my run would make him give ground.

It was a miscalculation. Peter blocked hard and knocked me back. I went down into the mud and slid.

My knee and arm stung, but I couldn't pay attention to it. I got up again as fast as I could and faced Dad. I knew it looked bad. I couldn't let it stop me.

He just looked at me as though he'd proven his point and there was no more to say. Without another word, ball in hand, he headed back to the house.

"I can do this!" I shouted after him as I jumped in front and tried to take the ball from him. "Let me show you."

He held the ball high so I couldn't reach it. "It's very simple," he said calmly. "You're not tough enough. Those guys will destroy you."

That was it. I couldn't hold back the tears anymore. The frustration and anger I felt made me feel close to exploding. I punched Dad angrily and let my tears flow without even trying to stop them.

"Gracie, stop!" he said. There was kindness in his voice, but I didn't want to know about it. He tried to hug me. I just pushed him away. I couldn't be hugged by him, the man who didn't care about my hopes and dreams.

He went inside, followed by Mike and Daniel. Peter waited for me there in the rain. I wasn't in the mood to talk to him, though. I'd told him to play hard, but did he have to play that hard? "Get out of here!" I shouted at him, still seething, my arms and knees stinging.

I was still standing there in the rain when his car pulled out of the driveway. Dad left next. Good. I didn't want to see any of their smirking, self-satisfied boy faces.

After a few minutes, Mom came out to the stoop. "Get cleaned up. You can ride with me," she offered.

I figured I might as well go to school as hang around the house. I wiped the mud off with a towel, pulled on any old dry jeans and shirt, and, not even bothering to brush out my hair, got into the car with her.

As she drove, I tried to focus all my attention on the windshield wipers going back and forth…back and forth. That way I wouldn't have to think about anything else.

After a couple of blocks, Mom broke the silence. "Not everything is possible," she said.

"It was for Johnny," I replied sullenly.

"It's different for you. You're a girl," she insisted.

I'd heard her say stuff like this before, and it made me crazy. She was always telling me how her mother said women have it tougher and had to accept life's unfairness. Didn't she know there was a women's movement going on, that women were protesting and marching, trying to change things? I'd never thought too much about it because I never thought it had anything to do with me. But at least I knew it was going on! What world did she live in?

"You didn't have to take his side," I mumbled, turning away from her.

Six

The next six months were sort of a blur. I guess I went to school and all, but I was numb inside. Everything seemed to be going on in some other world outside of me. I was far away from it all. It was better that way. Being removed from the world meant I didn't have to care about anything or feel anything or even think about anything.

I still thought about Johnny, of course. I thought about him every day when I fed his hawk, which I took into my room. The bird still wasn't able to fly. I'd let him out of the cage, but he only hopped around. In my secret opinion, he wasn't going to fly again. But I knew Johnny had thought he would, so I never said it out loud.

Time seemed to pass in its everyday sort of way, but I drifted through most of it in a haze. I remember one day sitting in class, staring out the window while Mr. Clark, my history teacher, rattled on about Lincoln or someone, and I was surprised to realize that there were buds on the trees. Spring was coming. It sort of took me by surprise.

The bell for the end of class rang and I was preparing to bolt, but Mr. Clark caught my eye. "Ms. Bowen, a moment, please."

This couldn't be good.

"Your exam surprised me," he said. "It was blank."

What could I say? My mind had been blank when I took the exam. Blank was my new favorite state of mind. I knew he expected some kind of explanation but once again I was...*blank*.

"What do you think I should do? Fail you?" he pressed.

He was a nice man and probably not a bad teacher, if I ever bothered to listen in class. He was the assistant soccer coach, and Johnny had always said he was cool. In some faraway part of my mind, I longed to tell him how cut off I felt, how I just couldn't seem to care about anything. But I couldn't reach that part of me, couldn't make it speak—so I just stood there, staring, not knowing what to say or even able to try very hard.

"Gracie, I'll overlook this—but you'll need to step up for the next one," he said.

He expected me to promise I would try. I didn't want to make him a promise I had no intention of keeping. "I've got to get going," I said instead.

His frustration was written all over his face. "Do you want to talk to someone, maybe the nurse?" he suggested.

"My mother *is* the nurse," I reminded him flatly.

"I knew your brother...you could talk to me," he said kindly. I really wished I *could,* but I couldn't talk to anyone.

Jena was waiting for me outside the door. There were some things I *could* talk to her about, not the things deep inside like the blank thing, but lighter stuff like school and guys. She was always interested in talking about guys.

I had pretty big news so, with a jerk of my head, I indicated that we should go to our special spot behind the bleachers. It was where we went to talk about things we didn't want anyone to overhear.

"Kyle's going to be captain next year," I told her when we got there. It wasn't my really big news. I was holding back on that.

"He told you that?" she asked, impressed.

"Yeah, when I told him I'd go out with him." It had happened just two days earlier. He had cornered me on my way out of gym and told me he had big news that he'd reveal only if I agreed to go out with him. It surprised me because I thought he'd forgotten about me. To be honest, I'd forgotten about him, but I remembered how hot I always thought he was as he stood there with that confident look on his face. So I agreed. "He's going to pick me up tonight at seven."

"What are you going to do?" Jena asked.

I shrugged. "He didn't say."

She gave me a look and I shot one back to her. We both knew Kyle was the make-out king of Columbia High. I could handle him, keep him at bay, but maybe I didn't want to. I hadn't made up my mind yet.

In the distance, we heard the bell for the next class. "I can't miss bio again," she said, picking up her books to go.

"I can," I said, sitting on the grass as Jena headed back to the school building. Skipping class had become one of my favorite pastimes. Besides, I wanted to think about Kyle and our date that night.

Getting Mom and Dad to agree to let me go wasn't going to be easy. Dad never spoke well of Kyle as a player. He thought he was a glory hog, not a team player, which was true—and I was pretty sure Dad wouldn't want me going out with him. But I had learned strategy from playing soccer. If I couldn't get directly past a player, I could try to get around him.

*

That night, to everyone's surprise, we found out that Mom had done the unthinkable. She'd cleaned out Johnny's room, packed away his trophies, plaques, photos, and posters. She'd stripped his bed and emptied his closets and dressers. "We need the space. It's been months," she told Dad with a little crack of sorrow in her voice. "I knew if I asked, you'd never say okay."

She'd been right about that. He just turned around and went into his room, slamming the door angrily behind him.

I understood exactly how he felt. I couldn't believe she'd done it, either. It was Johnny's room! Johnny was still part of our family! She couldn't take his room away!

Daniel and Mike immediately began squabbling over who would get the room. Would they ever stop being such little monsters?

I went back to my room and shut the door, locking it, wanting to block out my whole family. I turned the radio on high so I wouldn't even have to hear them. Pulling open my top drawer I took out some Saltines and fed them to Johnny's hawk for a treat. Maybe it was my way of saying sorry to Johnny about his room.

I let the hawk out of the cage and stroked the top of his soft head lightly with my fingertips. I had a secret I would never tell anyone because they would think I was insane: I liked to think that Johnny's soul had gone into this hawk. Sometimes the hawk looked at me with his deep yellow eyes and I was sure it was true. Whether it was true or not, it made me happy to think it.

From down the hall, I heard Mom and Dad arguing. Their bedroom door slammed. Dad's heavy footsteps stomped down the stairs. That would make my exit strategy more complicated.

It was almost seven and I couldn't wait to get out of here. I decided not to ask my parents for permission to go out with Kyle, in case they said no. I was going, no matter what, so it would be easier if I just didn't ask. That way they couldn't say I had disobeyed them. I'd say I didn't know it was such a big deal. That would be a lie, of course, but I didn't care, really.

Finally, I heard a horn honk outside. It was Kyle in his souped-up GTO convertible, its engine revving. So cool! I grabbed my jacket and bag, turned off the radio, and stuck my head out into the hall. No one was there, so I sneaked down the stairs.

Peering over the banister, I saw Dad in the den watching sports on TV. I'd have to get through the hall right past him, but when he was involved in a game, he tuned everything else out. I hoped he was deep enough into it to be in that zoned-out sports haze. Since Johnny died he'd become even more oblivious to everything around him than even in the past, so my chances were good. As long as he hadn't heard Kyle honk or noticed him revving his engine outside, I might make it.

Barely breathing, I sort of glided to the front door. Dad didn't look up. I winced as I unlatched the front lock. *Was it always so loud?* I slipped out and pulled the door shut behind me. The closing click seemed to bang like thunder.

I waited a moment—and then finally exhaled. No one was following me out. I'd made it.

Kyle was at the curb, grinning.

As I'd planned, I pulled off the big shirt I had on over the tight tee beneath it and yanked my hair out of its ponytail, letting it fall below my shoulders. I was ready for my big date with Kyle.

I headed for the passenger side and got in. The car was moving before I even shut the door.

Seven

"Pull over," I told Kyle when we were in the S-curve overpass outside town. Without even looking at me, he pulled right off the road. It wasn't the most private make-out spot on earth, what with cars zooming by, but I guess he figured it was the one I'd picked, so he'd happily go along with it.

He was wrong, though. Even though I thought Kyle was incredibly attractive, making out with him wasn't what I had in mind right then. I still hadn't made up my mind about how I wanted to handle that. But I didn't quite know how to tell him what I *did* have in mind.

I knew we'd drive through here—you sort of had to in order to get out of town—and there was something I'd wanted to do for a long time, but I needed someone with a car in order to carry it out. Jena didn't have one and neither did I, and it wasn't the kind of thing my parents, or even Peter, would have approved of. So when Kyle came along, it was the perfect opportunity.

Kyle had moved in close and was running his fingers along the line of my necklace. "Your skin is so soft," he said in kind of a dreamy way. As he moved in for a kiss, I slid back and out the passenger-side door. "Where are you goin'?" he cried.

He'd see for himself in a minute. There were no cars coming, so I darted across the road to the cement divider that separated the outgoing and incoming traffic. Once I was safely there, I pulled a can of red spray paint from my bag. I'd had it in there for weeks, determined to be ready if I had the chance to do this.

Kyle got out of the car and stood by the hood. "Gracie?!" he called. He was completely confused, and I couldn't blame him. He started to cross to me, but I was already heading to the other side. I wanted everyone coming into town to see what I was going to write: J. B. Johnny Bowen.

"Whoeee!" Kyle cheered from the divider as I began to spray the initial on the inside of the wall, just near the entrance. "Your G is backward," he added.

"It's a J, for Johnny," I called back, still working.

"Hey, yeah. That's really, really sweet," he said, sounding disappointed. I realized then that he thought I was spraying *our* initials, his and mine, onto the wall. What kind of a lovesick wimp did he think I was? I knew he thought a lot of himself, but that was a bit much. This was only our first date, after all.

Kyle was impatiently waiting for his make-out session. When I got back to the car, his arms were instantly around me and he kissed me hard. I wasn't feeling it and I tried to put him off, but it only made him mad. So I got out of the car and started walking. He drove alongside and told me to get in. When I didn't, he sped away.

It would be cool to have been Kyle's girlfriend. My social status would instantly rise to the level of a cheerleader. Girlfriend of a team captain is pretty high ranking. But I didn't care, just like I didn't care about anything else.

When I got home, I hoped I could sneak in the back door and get to my room without anyone knowing I had ever been out of the house. But when I arrived in the yard, I didn't want to go in.

I wanted to play soccer.

The one thing I *did* care about, nobody would let me do.

Well, I was going to practice, right then and there. I turned on the night spotlights, not caring who knew I was outside. I grabbed a ball and began dribbling it up and down the yard. Then I shot and landed it right in the broken-down goal. I dribbled it back out, shot, and scored again.

After a while, Dad came to the window, probably wondering why the lights were on. In their glare, he didn't see me. Nothing new there. He *never* saw me—not really.

I shot the ball into the goal. "I *am* tough enough!" I said to him, even though he couldn't hear me.

This time something inside me was different. I knew he couldn't hear me, as always, only I no longer cared.

*

At six the next morning, my clock radio went off and Springsteen, my favorite, began singing "Growin' Up" in my ear. I'd set the clock early so I could get up and do crunches before school. If Dad wouldn't train me to play soccer, I'd train myself. Next, I pulled on sweats and went out for a jog.

After only three weeks of doing this, I started seeing a change in my body. My abs had always been flat; now they were rock-hard. My calves began to bulge from the daily jog or bike ride.

I was getting there but not fast enough, so I stepped up my routine. After school I dribbled a soccer ball up a steep hill in the park. I installed a chin-up bar in my closet and began working on that. I was terrible at it, dropping to the floor after only three pull-ups.

I had to make my arms much stronger, and I thought I knew how to achieve that. The next morning, I got up even earlier so I could ride my bike to school. The super was just unlocking the side door when I got there, and I slipped in behind him.

By the time Coach Colasanti got to his office outside the weight room that morning, I had been working on lifting weights for a half hour. "The weight room doesn't open until eight," he told me gruffly. "And it's for boys only."

I didn't stop lifting. "Are those written policies or just common practice?" I asked. I had prepared this remark ahead of time, knowing the coach would object to my being there.

The coach glanced at me and started picking things up around the room, putting weights in order, throwing old towels in a bin. He wasn't kicking me out, so I figured I'd try to get his permission. "The girls' gym has no weights," I pointed out. "I could be here early. No one would know."

"I'd know," he replied.

"Is that such a burden?" I asked. Deep down, I knew Coach Colasanti liked me. He loved Johnny and knew my family. Besides, he liked anybody who liked soccer as much as the members of my family did.

He didn't reply, but I knew I could use the weight room as long as no one else found out about it.

It took some more weeks of pumping iron, but soon I could do five, then ten chin-ups on my bar. The work was paying off.

One night I stood in front of my mirror in my sleeveless nightgown and looked at my body. I flexed my arm and a very definite bicep appeared. Pounding my midsection, I could feel that it was rock-solid. I was looking good!

Eight

One afternoon after I trained hard, I came home to find Peter out in the yard training with Mike and Daniel. I was drinking a glass of water and watching them through the kitchen window when Mom came in, loaded down with groceries. "Why is Peter here?" I asked her.

"The boys wanted someone to practice with," she said as she started putting away the food.

I turned my back to the window, angry. They couldn't practice with me? They were just as bad as Dad. It was no surprise. He trained them to be that way.

"Want to go with me Saturday?" Mom offered. She touched the ends of my hair. "A trim would get that hair off your face."

I jerked away from her. What was this—Remind Grace She's a Girl Day? "I like my hair," I snapped at her.

"All right, then, we can stop at the mall for some new tops," she offered. Something was going on with her and I didn't know what. Money was tight at our house. Why did she suddenly want to spend money on me? "I don't like the clothes there," I grumbled.

"Okay," she said, sounding a little frustrated. "You choose something we can do together. Anything you want."

What I wanted was to get away from her. She was acting too weird. I tried to escape into the dining room, but she trailed behind me. "Why are you so angry?" she demanded.

I whirled around to face her. "I'm busy," I said, practically spitting out the words. It would have been too much to have expected her to notice what I was doing. She could have asked me how the training was going, or *why* I was training. No, instead she criticized my hair and tried to divert me to a mall crawl, something more acceptable for a girl to be doing. I was so sick of nobody in my family knowing who I was!

"What are you busy with?" she demanded angrily. "A boy?"

I threw my hands in the air, giving up. She was unbelievable. In her mind if I wasn't interested in my hair or shopping, the only other thing that could be occupying my mind had to be a boy! "Just things," I said sarcastically as I walked away from her. "You know!"

"I don't know," she shouted at my back. "That's why I'm asking. We saw Mr. Clark and Mr. Enright today."

Mr. Enright?

That stopped me cold just as I was about to head up the stairs.

Mr. Enright was the principal of the school. And she'd said "we." Had Dad gone, too?

I turned toward her just as Dad walked into the dining room. "Grace, you're flunking history," he said. "Mr. Clark knows you cheated from Jena on the last test. Your answers were identical, even the wrong ones. Your grade right now is zero!"

This was about as bad as it could get. In my house, cheating on a test was an even bigger offense than failing. In fact, it was huge. But I'd done it and not very well, apparently. What I didn't want to do was have a big endless conversation about how they were so disappointed in me. I didn't care. Nothing mattered anymore. "So I'm grounded? What?" I asked.

"I didn't say that. Not yet, anyway," Dad replied.

What could they really do to me? There was nothing they could take away that I would care about. I knew it and so did they. I didn't want to stand around and hear them blab about it. "Let me know when you decide something," I said, heading up the stairs.

In my room, I took out Johnny's old hand weights, sat on my bed, and began to lift. There was a knock on the door and I knew it was Dad from the sound of it. Quickly, I slid the weights under my bed. Without waiting for an answer, he stepped inside. "What's going on?" he demanded.

Nothing was going on. I didn't want to be in school. It was just a lot of useless facts to learn, more meaningless junk. I couldn't tell him that, though, so I just sat there in silence.

"Do I have to check your homework every night?" he asked. "If you're going to act like a kid, that's how I'm going to treat you."

I just turned away from him. I knew this would really get him mad, but I couldn't think of anything else to do.

"Okay, show me your homework," he insisted, his voice rising.

"Haven't done it," I muttered.

"Do it now!"

"Can't," I said. "I didn't bring my books home." I cringed just a little as I spoke because I knew I was pushing him over the edge of his patience, and I was right.

"You're grounded!" he exploded. "Come home straight from school."

No big deal. Most of my workouts were in the morning, and afterward I could still exercise in my room.

"If those grades don't go up—summer school!" he added, then slammed the door on the way out.

Summer school! Ow! I had to give him credit. I hadn't thought of that.

*

So even though the days were getting warmer and longer and nicer, I came home dutifully after school and went inside. I did my crunches and chin-ups and lifted weights in my room, still determined that some way, somehow, I would find my chance to prove that I could play soccer as well as any boy.

In my spare time, I opened a textbook or two. It wasn't that I had developed a sudden love of learning. It was just that summer school would seriously interrupt

60

the months that I was counting on for maximum training time.

One afternoon I came home on my bike and found
Dad out in the yard kicking a soccer ball around with
Peter, Mike, and Daniel. I guessed he'd gotten off from
work early for some reason. What struck me was the
unfairness of it. I should have been playing with them.
Why wasn't I?

I was walking past them toward the back door when
something happened I couldn't resist. Daniel lost the ball
and it rolled right in front of me. Without even thinking,
I stole it away.

"Gracie!" Dad cried, annoyed.

Peter was instantly beside me, trying to steal it back.
He might not have been playing as hard as he could, but
I was. There was no way he was getting the ball back.

In a second, Dad was beside Peter. They were double-
teaming! Dad knocked me off the ball with a shoulder
charge. That was so like him. He *would* play just as rough
as he could to get rid of me!

Furious, I charged at him and got the ball back. Yes!
I pushed it right, then left, cutting back, and then turning fast, heading for the goal! "Peter, cover her!" Dad
shouted.

It was too late. BAM! I shot it right into the goal!

What would Dad say to *that?*

I waited to hear. I could see how impressed Peter was.
Even my monstrous little brothers were staring at me
with their mouths agape.

But Dad said nothing as he picked up the ball. Well, he did say *something:* "Okay, back to work."

I had promised myself I wouldn't care what he said, or did, or thought—not anymore. At that moment, I nearly broke that promise to myself. If one of the boys had done what I just did, he would at least have said, "Good job." But he wouldn't say it to me.

Well, it was fine. It was just fine. I didn't need him or anybody.

In the kitchen, I saw that my leg was bleeding. Peter had probably gotten me with his cleat. At the time I hadn't even noticed. I tore off a corner of a paper towel and stuck it on to dab up the blood. Mom handed me a box of Band-Aids, but I pushed them away.

"Take them," she insisted. "You need shin guards."

"You never cared when I played with Johnny," I reminded her.

"Johnny protected you," she replied in a matter-of-fact tone.

Had he? I never realized it. That would have been just like Johnny to take care of me and make me think I was doing it myself. Was that why none of them thought I could take care of myself now?

After washing the cut and putting on the Band-Aid, I settled into a seat by an open window that overlooked the backyard to watch them finish playing. If I couldn't join in, I could at least get the benefit of Dad's coaching.

When they were done, Dad, Daniel, and Mike went inside. Peter was about to leave when he noticed me and came over. "Hey," he said, "Friday we meet up at the old stadium for pickup games."

At first I didn't understand; then I realized. He was inviting me to go. The flicker of excitement I felt quickly died out as I remembered that I was grounded. "I can't go—anywhere," I told him glumly.

"Can't—or won't?" he asked.

I turned away from him and when I turned back, he was gone.

Gracie Bowen (Carly Schroeder)
[All photos by K. C. Bailey/A Picturehouse Release]

The Columbia High soccer team, with Johnny Bowen (Jesse Lee Soffer) second from the left, wearing the Number 7 jersey.

Bryan Bowen (Dermot Mulroney) at the podium during the soccer awards dinner, holding Johnny's jersey, with Coach Colasanti (John Doman) listening on the left.

Left to right: Mike Bowen (Hunter Schroeder), Daniel Bowen (Trevor Heins), and Peter (Joshua Caras) doing soccer drills in the Bowen backyard as Bryan Bowen (Dermot Mulroney) coaches them.

Peter (Joshua Caras, *left)* and Gracie (Carly Schroeder, *right)* chase a ball as Bryan Bowen (Dermot Mulroney, *center)* watches from the goal area.

Left to right: Mike (Hunter Schroeder) and his mom, Lindsay Bowen (Elisabeth Shue)

Gracie (Carly Schroeder) and
her father (Dermot Mulroney)
get in some serious training.

Left to right: Bryan Bowen (Dermot Mulroney) and Lindsay Bowen (Elisabeth Shue) discuss Gracie with Coach Clark (Andrew Shue).

Left to right: Chairwoman Bowsher (Leslie Lyles), Lindsay Bowen (Elisabeth Shue), Gracie (Carly Schroeder), and Bryan Bowen (Dermot Mulroney) at the School Board hearing.

The Bowens *(left to right:* Elisabeth Shue, Carly Schroeder, and Dermot Mulroney) receive the good news that Gracie will be given a chance to try out for the soccer team.

Gracie (Carly Schroeder) has a grueling tryout as her best friend, Jena (Julia Garro), and the rest of her family (Hunter Schroeder, Elisabeth Shue, Trevor Heins, and Dermot Mulroney) watch the action.

Gracie (Carly Schroeder, *front)* walks by the cheerleaders *(left to right:* Emma Bell, Bernadette York, Jessica Asch, Amy Dannenmueller, Jennifer Garagano, and Karen Summerton) as they warm up.

Gracie (Carly Schroeder) on the bench at the big game.

Gracie (Carly Schroeder) takes a shot.

The cheerleaders at the game, screaming for Gracie *(left to right:* Bernadette York, Jennifer Garagano, Amanda Knox, Amy Dannenmueller, and Manting Chan).

Andrew Shue with the director (and brother-in-law) Davis Guggenheim

Davis Guggenheim setting up a shot.

Nine

Even though I was grounded, I knew Mom was taking the boys to the dentist that Friday and Dad wouldn't be home from work for a while. I took a chance and instead of going straight home after school, like I was supposed to, I took Peter up on his invitation to join the pickup game at the old stadium.

Jena came with me, always wanting to be anyplace where guys would be. "What did you tell your parents?" she asked as we walked to the field.

"About this? Nothing," I admitted.

I could see guys milling around, getting ready to play. I knew most of them from the team: Joe, Ben, Craig, Curt, and some others whose names I wasn't sure of.

Kyle approached from the opposite side of the field. The moment I saw him, I stopped and tensed up inside. Since our date-gone-wrong, I had discovered that he'd made bets with guys that he would score with me that night. When I found out about that, I was so glad I'd walked out of his car. I wondered if he'd told them the truth about it. Now he just glared at me whenever we passed in the hall in school.

"If you're going, go!" Jena said, nudging me with a small push. "Forget Kyle."

She was right. I'd come this far; I wasn't going to let Kyle turn me around now.

Kate Dorset and her cheerleader pals were nearby, sitting together in a group. Like Jena, they were never far from anywhere the guys were, the cute athletic ones, anyway.

As we got close, Jena sat down by herself, preparing to watch. I didn't see Peter, which made me even tenser. If I showed up wanting to play and nobody had invited me, I'd look like a real idiot. But then he stepped out from behind some guys, smiling. What a relief! "Gracie, you made it," he greeted me cheerfully. "Come on."

Peter guided me to the circle of guys getting ready to choose teams. The area where they planned to play was half grass, half cracked, broken asphalt—not exactly ideal.

They met my arrival with stony stares. Peter acted as if he didn't notice. "Gracie is going to play," he announced, as though they would think this was great news.

Kyle was the first to sneer at me. "This is a joke."

Peter and I looked at him but said nothing. He saw in an instant that it was no joke. "If that's what she wants, Peter, you take her," Kyle ordered.

Peter and a guy named Ronny were captains of one team. Kyle and Ben were captains of the other. With Peter as captain, at least I knew I'd get picked. That was the good news. The bad news was that Peter's team was definitely made up of players who were not as strong as those on Kyle's team.

Kyle kicked off and the game began. At first, I hung back a bit, too timid to jump in. Then it hit me that I was playing exactly as Dad predicted I would play, like a girl. So when Curt from our side got the ball, I moved into position to receive it. But even though I was in a much better spot, Curt passed it to Craig.

I stayed with the ball as we moved down the field with it, and eventually it came to me. This was my chance and I took it, running hard, determined to show them what I could do. Ben, the fullback from Kyle's team, came at me. Even though I was going at full speed, somehow he outran me and knocked me off the ball.

It wasn't long before they scored the first goal.

Begrudgingly, I saw what Dad had been getting at about the guys being stronger, heavier, and faster than me—even the new toned and super fit me. Playing soccer with my family hadn't prepared me for this level of tough competitive play. But strategy, speed, and skill had to count for something. I had those things. Practice and experience also counted, and that's what I *didn't* have. These guys played all the time. If I wanted to be as good as they were, I couldn't let them scare me off or I'd never get the practice.

In the next round of play, I made it my business to be tougher. I managed to cut the ball out from under Kyle, knocking him off his feet.

If Kyle didn't like me before this, I'm sure he hated me now. Kate and the cheerleaders giggled as he tumbled over. Even his teammates laughed.

I saw Kyle nod to Ben as he got to his feet. His angry glare said, *Get her.*

Ben charged at me, pushing me off the ball. I wasn't going to let him do it. I pushed back, hard, and got the ball back. He started hacking my ankles, cutting a gash with his cleats and knocking me backward to the ground as the ball disappeared up the field.

Kyle looked down at me, laughing coldly. He thought he'd gotten me back good and I guess he had. In an instant, though, I was on my feet, pushing him. Furious, I walked away and off the lousy makeshift field.

Peter ran after me. "Gracie, you can't go."

"I can't stay," I shouted. After this, Kyle's team would be all over me. They'd knock me down every chance they got.

What a jerk I'd been to think I could really do this! What a moron!

I stomped off the field, blind with anger and humiliation, not sure where I was going. Jena hurried behind me, but I was too beside myself to even speak. She stayed with me until I finally cooled down a little a few blocks from my house.

"Are you okay?" she asked, breathless from keeping up.

"You know what I want to do?" I asked. "I want to do something neither of us has ever done before, and I want to do it right now!"

"Why?" Jena asked. She was usually up for anything, but I think I was scaring her a little. Actually, I was scaring *me* a little. If I didn't get out of town that very minute, I felt that I would explode. I was sick of being Gracie Bowen, the girl who wanted to play soccer but couldn't. I wanted to be someone completely new.

*

It was late afternoon but still light when we got to the Jersey Shore in Mom's station wagon. I was going to catch hell for sneaking it out of the garage, especially considering I didn't have my license yet. I would definitely be in major trouble but, as with so much else, I didn't care.

What could happen? I wouldn't be playing soccer, it seemed. I was already grounded. I was possibly looking at months of summer school. If I didn't have some fun right then, I might not have another chance for a long time.

The boardwalk smelled like salt air, and I could hear the surf crashing not too far off. I was looking at a pair of sunglasses in a shop window when I realized Jena wasn't with me. I wasn't too worried; she'd probably stopped to check out a cute guy somewhere.

I saw her step out of a nearby shop with a strange look on her face, like she was pleased with herself but scared, too. "What?" I asked as she hurried toward me.

Without answering, she grabbed my arm and pulled me into an alley between shops. She'd shoplifted two bikini tops and two bottoms, one for each of us. I was horrified, then excited, and then thrilled.

We were walking on the wild side and tossing away the rulebook!

We found a public bathroom and put on the suits. Then we lay out on the beach until the sun was low in the sky and our skin felt scorched.

Farther up the beach at the clam bar, we spotted two cute guys. They were probably college kids down for spring break. We hung around nearby, smiling at them and flirting, until they finally invited us to sit down with them at the counter.

They ordered us all some beer and fried clams, which meant they were over eighteen and could drink. They seemed to assume we were old enough, too, and we didn't bother to tell them any differently.

On the deck, a band of guys was playing country music. The cuter of the two guys, Rob, asked Jena to dance with him. Out on the dance area they put their arms around each other and swayed to the music, both appearing slightly unsteady.

That left me alone with the guy named Adam. When Jena and Rob began kissing on the dance floor, it got sort of awkward sitting there watching them. Adam suggested we go for a walk along the beach. We walked for a while as the sun set. Adam kept asking me questions that I sensed were meant to help him find out whether I was over eighteen. I did my best not to give him a direct answer to any of them.

I was feeling the effects of the beer, and I wanted to keep on being the wild girl I'd set out to be: the new, care-free, wild Gracie Bowen. I suggested that we could sit in the back of my car if he wanted. He knew what I was suggesting and agreed right away.

It was nearly dark as we crawled into the backseat. He began kissing me, and I leaned back and let him. I wasn't madly in love with him or even wildly attracted to him. I hardly knew him! I had just never made out with a guy in the backseat of a car, and I knew a lot of girls had. I wanted to be like them, the other girls, not like me.

But my planned make-out session was abruptly interrupted by a glaring white light flooding the backseat.

Looking around Adam's shoulder, I saw Officer Sal staring down at me, aiming a flashlight in my face!

And then I was squinting up into the light at Dad!

Dad?

Was I having some kind of nightmare?!

Ten

Dad didn't go ballistic, as I'd expected. Instead, he seemed to want to talk. I didn't. "You can stop pretending you care now," I snarled at him, leaning against the passenger-side door, staring out into the darkness. "Nobody's watching!"

Maybe it was the beer making me so bold. Maybe it just made me sick that he'd made such a big show of coming to find his bad runaway daughter when normally he couldn't give me the time of day. What a hypocrite!

"Gracie, what the hell did you think you were doing?" he asked.

"Like you really want to have a conversation?" I shot back. If he did, it would have been the first time ever, at least with me.

"I do," he insisted.

"Go ahead, talk," I challenged him.

He opened his mouth but no words came out. I knew he couldn't do it—wouldn't do it. How could he possibly talk to me? I was a girl, and now I was a bad girl. Why should he waste his breath talking to me?

We drove in silence for the rest of the trip. He only spoke again to tell me that Jena's parents had also come to take her home. When we came in the back door, Mom was waiting. "You're okay?" she checked anxiously.

"Fine," I replied coolly.

Johnny's cleats and his hawk were on the kitchen table. They'd been looking around in my room! "You touched my stuff!" I accused angrily, grabbing the cage and heading up to my room.

It had been a very long day and, what with the beer and all, I was asleep in two seconds.

I *felt* as though I'd been asleep exactly ten minutes, though it had really been longer, when I was awakened by a wash of dawn light in my face. Dad had pulled open the drapes.

Was he crazy!? I rolled to the edge of my bed to escape the light.

"Don't make me get ice water," he said. Whatever he was up to, he meant business.

*

We were waiting at Coach Colasanti's office before he even got there. He wasn't surprised to see me, but he was puzzled by Dad's appearance. "Grace wants to play Varsity soccer," Dad announced.

I looked up at him, shocked. He hadn't said a word the whole trip over. I figured he was going to tell the coach not to let me use the weight room anymore. This was the last thing I'd expected, especially after yesterday.

Coach Colasanti unlocked his office and gestured for us to come in and sit down. He opened his container of coffee and took a sip before speaking. "That's terrific, really great, but Columbia doesn't have a girls' team," he replied.

"That's why she's trying out for the boys' team," Dad came back at him.

"No, I'm not," I jumped in. My game at the old stadium had proved to me that I wasn't nearly good enough. Dad held his hand up to me, telling me to stop talking and listen.

"I can't have a girl playing on a boys' team," the coach insisted.

"There's no law *against* it," Dad said.

"There's no law *for* it," Coach Colasanti countered. "She could get injured."

"So could any boy," Dad pointed out.

The coach sipped his coffee and took a moment to think about Dad's words. Then he shook his head. "I'm not risking the success of my team for one girl. We have the team this year to win the whole thing—"

"Grace could help you get there," Dad interrupted him. "Have you seen her play?"

My head snapped around as I looked at him in amazement. This was a first! Never before had he even hinted that he thought I was a good player!

"We're not asking for special treatment, just a tryout," Dad continued.

Coach Colasanti looked at me with doubt in his eyes.

"She can either do it or she can't," Dad pressed.

Coach Colasanti pushed back in his chair. "Anyway, it's not my call. Take it up with the School Board."

Dad nodded and got up, thanking the coach for his time. I followed him out of the gym. When we were in the hall, I exploded: "What the hell was that about?"

"You wanted to play, so let's petition the Board," he said.

He'd forgotten one little detail. I had flunked history. There were a couple more weeks of school, but not enough time to reverse it. "Too little too late," I reminded him as I turned to walk away.

"You'll do summer school in the morning and train in the afternoon," he said. "We've got months until tryouts."

I just didn't get him. Now he was all gung ho to train me? Why? "Where were you when I begged you?" I asked angrily. "Where have you been my whole life? Everything's always been about Johnny, about your *boys!* You never loved me! Do you even know who I am?"

We stared at each other. It was all out now. I'd said what I really felt—and he had no reply. I knew he wouldn't, so I turned to walk away.

"Gracie!" he shouted when I was nearly down the hall.

He wanted me to do what he said, to stop being such a pain and do it his way. He always wanted *everything* his way. Well, not this time. "No!" I shouted back at him. "I'm not good enough!"

"Do you think anyone gets good on their own?" he asked, coming toward me. So he *had* noticed that I was training myself. I hadn't realized he paid even that much attention to what I did. "I *coached* Johnny," he said.

"Johnny was a *natural,*" I said bitterly, repeating what I'd heard him say a thousand times.

"Johnny was a boy," he said.

I didn't want to hear any more about how Johnny was a boy and I wasn't. There was nothing more to say about it. I was right near the girls' room, the one place Dad couldn't follow me, so I bolted inside.

Standing by the door, breathing hard from emotion, I listened while Dad kept talking to me from the other side. "I didn't have anyone who cared," he said. "No one took the damn time. Maybe I wouldn't have screwed up my knee. Maybe I could've gone on with my game."

Tears came to my eyes. He'd never talked to me like this, never shared much of anything about his past. It had hurt me that he thought I was so unimportant. Now he was trying, though. He *was* trying.

"Gracie, I honestly don't know if you're good enough," he continued. "Let me help you."

Tears rolled down my cheeks. He stopped talking and waited. All I had wanted was a chance. I supposed he was only asking for a chance, too.

But was it too late for both of us?

Maybe so. It felt too late.

Footsteps in the hallway told me he had given up waiting for me to come out. I heard the sound of the exit door as he pushed it open.

Could I move from my spot? I didn't know.

And then I was out the door and running after him. I caught up on the cement path as he headed for his car. We walked the rest of the way side by side, not talking. I had to go to school, but I went as far as the car.

If he was willing to take a chance on me, I'd give him the chance to do it.

Eleven

Dad and I started training hard. He got me up early and we worked until after dark.

Dad was tough, but guess what? I was tougher. I was just a hair better, but there were times I left him panting, struggling to keep up with me. This shocked me and I think, from the look on his face, it took him by surprise, too.

In a way, our daily training sessions became a battle of wills. Neither one of us wanted to admit that the training was torture. We both acted like it was a piece of cake; though I don't know what kind of cake leaves you struggling to breathe and feeling like you might vomit at any moment.

Mom, Mike, and Daniel thought we had lost our minds. "Delusional" is what Mike called us. It occurred to me that he might be right.

*

One night, I heard Mom and Dad arguing. Since Johnny died, they fought more than they ever had before. It was almost as if they blamed each other for his death, though I don't see how either of them could possibly have been to blame for such a stupid, tragic accident. My guess was that they felt that they had to blame someone. I knew because I'd felt the same way. My parents just turned that need to blame against each other.

This conversation, though, was different. It was quiet and intense, as though the subject was so serious they couldn't risk any of us kids hearing. I was in the dining room, though, and I could hear them talking in the kitchen. Mom asked Dad why his paychecks weren't showing up in their bank account.

"I quit my job," he told her.

At first Mom didn't say anything. She must have been as stunned as I was. Quit his job?

"When?" she asked him after a moment.

Dad didn't answer.

"Without discussing it?" Mom asked indignantly.

"I couldn't tell you," Dad replied. I wondered if Dad felt the same way I did, if Johnny's death had made him simply stop caring. Just as I couldn't care about school, maybe he couldn't bring himself to care about his job anymore. I understood that.

"I need a break," he insisted. "I'll find something new."

"What are we going to live on?" Mom demanded.

"Right now, I'm coaching Grace," he replied firmly. "I'm not losing another kid."

The back door slammed shut as he went out into the yard, ending their conversation.

I sat there thinking about what I'd heard. It was a lot to take in. I knew Mom was right to worry about how we'd live, but that wasn't the main thing on my mind. The thing that really grabbed me was that Dad was putting my training before his job. He was going to give it everything he had—everything.

It meant I couldn't let him down, not even for a second. I promised myself, then and there, that I wouldn't.

*

So the training continued. Even though my brothers still thought we were "delusional," they helped me repair the goal Dad had torn down on the day of Johnny's funeral.

Dad put together a weight room in the garage. He got a lot of the equipment from stuff he'd found during bulk pickup day, when people put out their big furniture and anything else big that they wanted the garbage trucks to take away. "It's amazing what people throw away," he commented as he dragged in a leg-press weight board.

I figured part of not letting Dad down was to avoid summer school if at all humanly possible, and I wasn't sure that it was. Summer school would eat up precious time that we needed to train if I was going to be ready for tryouts in September. With all my class cuts, the blank test, and the zero for cheating, my current grade was completely in the toilet. But Mr. Clark was a decent guy, and I had to give it a try.

One day after class, I approached him. "I need to pick up my grade," I said. "Can I write a paper or something?"

He handed me a textbook about the Civil War. "Read a chapter every day. Summarize it and bring me your summary at each class," he said.

A few weeks earlier I would have just walked away from an assignment like that. Now I had a reason to be happy about it. He was giving me a chance, and I appreciated it. "I'll be here," I assured him with a smile.

"With your summaries," he emphasized.

I nodded, thanking him as I backed out the door. If I had to read the chapters in the middle of the night with a flashlight, I was determined to get the summaries done and avoid summer school.

*

Dad and I trained well into the evenings. Some nights he put on the big outdoor lights and I ran through a tight obstacle course of orange cones that he'd set up. I was slowly improving, each night knocking over fewer and fewer of them.

Sometimes I played scrimmages with Mike and Daniel while Dad coached from the side, just as he'd done with Johnny.

Mom wasn't home in the evenings anymore because she'd picked up a second job at the hospital. In the mornings, she looked tired. It wasn't easy on her. I knew she was doing it so Dad could train me without worrying about looking for work. She was another person I couldn't let down.

One evening, while we ate frozen dinners Dad had heated up, he set up his reel-to-reel projector and the stand-up screen. He put on a movie of a soccer game. "Is that Johnny?" I asked, seeing a player who looked a lot like him.

"It's me," Dad said.

I leaned in, looking closer. It *was* Dad at about nineteen, dressed in a soccer uniform and playing in one of his college games.

"It was my junior year," he said. "You've seen this before."

I shook my head. "Never." He might have shown Johnny, but I would have remembered if I'd ever seen it.

"This was before I hurt my knee," he added, leaning back in his chair to watch the play on the screen. "Watch this. Wait, wait…now! Ooooh! I smoked that guy!"

"You were, like, a star!" Mike cheered.

"Hardly," Dad told him. "Mostly I warmed the bench."

It surprised me to hear him admit that. I had always assumed he had been a big-shot soccer player in college. We all had.

"I had no one watching out for me," Dad said as an explanation.

"What about Granddad?" I asked.

Dad turned away sadly. "What about him?" he asked. I suddenly realized that I wasn't the only one who had ever felt all alone. Dad had done it on his own, and it hadn't turned out as he'd hoped.

I recalled him saying that nobody got there on their own. He must have been thinking about his own life. Was that why he coached Johnny so hard? Was he trying to give him something he'd never had? Had he only lately realized that a daughter might need his help as much as a son?

Even if it was a little late, he'd realized it in time. I wasn't going it alone anymore. I had to admit it felt good.

*

My training put a strain on my friendship with Jena. She'd been grounded because of the Jersey Shore escapade, but when she was free again, she wanted to hang out like we used to. I no longer had the time, though.

"People are talking," she said to me one day while I was training in the garage weight room. "You're committing social suicide."

"Like I care," I said, still lifting.

Dad came in with two cartons of eggs. Jena rolled her eyes at him as she walked out in a huff. I didn't blame her for being angry. She felt like I'd abandoned her. If she was really my friend, though, she had to understand how much this meant to me.

Dad stood before me and I saw that he had no shoes on. He tossed an egg lightly into the air and, when it came down, he caught it on the toes of his right foot. "Soft as a pillow," he remarked before tossing it up again with his right foot and catching it with his left.

I was impressed.

He gestured for me to stand and take off my shoes. "I'm going to toss you this little guy. Catch him on your foot and cradle him. Don't break him."

There was no way I could do that! I tried anyway, but as I'd expected, it broke, making a gooey mess all over my bare foot. "It didn't work," I said, pointing out the obvious.

"You didn't do it right" was all he said. He tossed another into the air for me to catch. It made another yellow, yolky mess at my feet.

"It's impossible," I wailed.

"I know," he agreed, tossing a third egg into the air. "Again."

The egg tossing went on for the rest of the afternoon. I didn't catch one of them.

Catching the egg became an obsession with me. I knew it killed Mom to see all those eggs going to waste, and I appreciated that she didn't complain. One Saturday afternoon we were out on the front porch together. I was trying to catch an egg while she folded laundry. "I haven't seen Jena in a while," she commented.

"Me, neither," I said, sadly. *Splat!* The broken egg slid down the porch steps. Mom gave a look and sighed, but she didn't say a word.

As she walked away with the basket of laundry, I tried one more egg.

Got it!

Yes!

Twelve

Now the trick was to get it every time. That would take practice.

It wasn't easy throwing and catching on my own. I needed someone to throw for me. I couldn't ask Mom, and Dad had taken Mike and Daniel to another dentist appointment. It wasn't something I could ask Jena to do, either. There was only one person who might be home and might be willing: Peter.

I walked to his house, which was only around the corner. I knew where he lived, but I hadn't been there in years. When I got there, he was in his garage, which was set up for a garage band. I didn't even know he played. "Hi," I said, feeling sort of funny. "I should have called, but then I realized I've never called you. So here I am."

He was surprised to see me but he smiled, waiting for me to explain why I was there. I held up my carton of eggs. "You cooking something?" he asked.

"Nope. Toss me one," I said, handing him the carton. He looked really confused as he took out one of the eggs. "Go ahead," I prodded him as I slipped out of my flip-flops. "Toss it to me."

He tossed it and I missed, making a big yellow mark on his driveway. "Again," I requested.

Peter glanced around at his parents' nice car parked nearby. "Careful," he said nervously. He tossed the egg and I missed. Some of it splattered onto the car.

"Forget the car," Peter said, and we both laughed. He took off his sneakers and wanted to try. As I had, he missed at first, but it didn't take him as long as it had taken me to start catching them. Soon we were tossing them back and forth with our bare feet there in his driveway.

"Do you think I have a chance at the boys' Varsity team?" I asked.

"At trying out or making the team?" he asked, catching an egg with his feet.

"How would the other guys feel?" I asked.

"Worried about all of them or just one?" he countered. We both knew he was talking about Kyle. "Just be a great player," he advised.

"I'm going to be better than you," I warned him, keeping the egg volley going.

"That won't be too hard," he said with a grin.

I admired that he could joke about the fact that he never made first-string. He was on the bench most of the time. "You stay on the team—why?" I asked as gently as I could. I didn't want to hurt his feelings, but I was curious.

"Because my dad thinks I should quit," he joked.

I shot him a disbelieving look. That couldn't possibly be the only reason.

"I play because there's always next year, and I'm an optimist," he amended, more honestly this time.

The egg that we'd kept going for a good five minutes shattered right between us. "Not a bad run," he said, taking another one out of the carton.

"Not bad at all," I agreed. I was seeing him in a new light, maybe really seeing him for the first time. He was thoughtful and funny, and a rebel in his own way. No wonder he'd been Johnny's best friend. "You're nice," I complimented him sincerely.

That made him smile. "I'm always nice—to you," he said.

It was true; he always had been nice to me—really nice. Why had I been so thick-headed that I'd never noticed it before?

We looked down at the sea of broken eggs around us. What a mess! I'd have to help him clean it up.

Peter looked at me with a serious expression. "If you're going to play with the guys, you need to train with them," he said.

At that moment, I got it. Dad was still not training me full out. He was probably afraid the boys would cream me, as they'd tried to do that day at the stadium. I now understood something about Dad that I hadn't known before. He wasn't holding back because he didn't believe in me, not entirely. He just didn't want me to get hurt—my feelings or my body. I didn't blame him anymore, but it was time to stop holding back. I *am* a much better player now.

I thanked Peter and headed for home. Dad was there. He had climbed a tall ladder to trim the front hedges.

The first thing I did was check the mailbox to see if I'd gotten anything from the School Board. I was waiting for a reply to my request to try out for the team. There was no letter from them.

The next thing I did was shoot a soccer ball right at Dad's ladder. "Watch it!" he shouted.

"Dad," I said, grinning up at him. "I'm ready."

"No, you're not," he said, going back to clipping the hedges.

"I'm ready for my real training," I explained.

He froze right there, knowing exactly what I meant. He must have been afraid this moment would come, and now it had. "I don't want to just stay alive out there," I said. "I want to know how to score, how to win."

I knew I was right. Dad knew it, too. Phase two of my soccer training was about to begin.

Thirteen

Summer came and summer school began. My extra work had been too little too late. Mr. Clark just couldn't find enough points to pass me. Even with my summer school work, I managed to take advantage of the extra daylight hours for training.

At my suggestion, Dad recruited Peter to help me. He was supposed to give me a taste of real play, but sometimes he just couldn't bring himself to be tough with me. "Peter!" Dad would scold him when he saw him going easy on me. "You're not helping anyone!"

After he was reprimanded, which seemed to happen at least once a session, Peter would play with everything he had. When he did, I couldn't touch him. And he was a guy who mostly warmed the bench!

"Be aggressive," Dad coached. "Think of the ball as life or death. You have to win it. You've got to *believe* you can take the ball."

I wanted to believe. I did believe. But it just didn't happen.

Dad was getting frustrated. "Help me out here," he said to me one day when Peter had taken the ball from me for about the tenth time. "Weren't you always playing with Johnny?"

"We fooled around," I replied. "We played for fun."

"You did drills?" he asked.

"We didn't call them that," I said.

Dad sighed, seemingly at a loss for what to do next. "How did you teach Johnny?" I asked.

"I didn't. He was a natural, remember?" Dad said.

Dad did everything he could think of to get me to be more aggressive. He and Peter even tried pushing me so I'd get mad and push back. I did get angry and shove, throwing my weight into them, but I could barely budge them. They were just bigger and heavier!

We kept working even after Peter had to go home. Dad tried another tactic. He concentrated on ways for me to get my opponent off balance, figuring that might equalize the difference in our sizes. "Get your opponent moving one way. Then, when his weight shifts, cut the ball," he instructed.

It would have worked, I suppose, but I couldn't get the timing right. I had to get the ball the moment the opponent shifted weight, and I always seemed to be a little behind or a little ahead.

Dad was trying everything he could think of, and his patience held out for a long time. Finally, though, he cracked. "Watch what I do and do it!" he shouted at me. He threw me the ball, and once again I headed for the goal. He barreled toward me, hitting me with his shoulder. I fell over onto my rear end, sliding in the dirt.

Mom must have been watching from the kitchen window and seen Dad knock me down. "Time to stop," she said, coming out onto the back stoop.

"In a minute," Dad told her.

She gestured toward me, sitting on the ground. "It's too much for her."

Her words made me get to my feet. "Does it look like it's too much?" Dad argued as I walked toward him. He tossed me the ball. "Try it again."

My hip hurt from the fall. The palms of my hands were scraped. But I felt happy, happy to be working so hard at something I cared so much about, happy to care about something again.

And, as frustrated as he was, Dad seemed happy, too. Soccer was what he loved and when he threw himself into it, he seemed most alive.

I don't think Mom was too happy, though. Mostly, she seemed worried, worried about me and about money. She seemed tired, too. She stood there that day watching us for another few minutes, and then she headed off for her second job at the hospital. In a way, this training was as hard on her as it was on Dad and me, maybe harder. I knew that if I succeeded—*when* I succeeded—I'd owe the success as much to her as to Dad.

That evening, Mike was setting up our frozen dinners on TV trays when I came into the room. "Dad found the movie reel with Pelé on it," he told me.

Instantly my mind flashed to the poster of the soccer star that had hung in Johnny's room. Dad had told me he'd once seen Pelé play and had filmed part of the game, though I'd never seen the actual film.

We got our suppers and Dad began the movie. Daniel banged my shoulder when Pelé came on. "See him?"

"Keep watching," Dad said to me. On the screen, Pelé was tracking a much bigger opponent. The player knocked him down, but Pelé sprang back up, stole the ball, and scored.

"Pelé wasn't tall or fast, but he had it up here," Dad said, tapping his forehead. "And he had it in here," he added, pointing to his heart. "He made the impossible possible." He turned his attention back to the screen. "Look how he absorbs that guy's energy and turns it on him!"

Dad got up and began to pace as he watched Pelé in action. "In every game there's one moment when one player can change everything. *Di momento de gracia.*"

Dad rewound the film and gestured for me to come beside him so we could look at it together. This time he ran the scene of Pelé taking the ball from the larger player in slow motion. "Right there, when that guy hesitates…that's the moment, when everything sets up perfect and then pauses. Pelé feels it."

I watched again as Pelé scored and his teammates went wild with joy.

"The moment of grace," Dad said. He turned to me. "It's where you got your name."

I looked up at him, totally surprised. No one had ever told me that about my name before.

He smiled at me. "It's how I felt the day you were born. I knew that anything was possible."

And all the while I had thought he hadn't even noticed.

*

After I saw the film of Pelé, something clicked in my
head. I got it. I saw what he was doing. Not that there
wasn't still a ton of work to do. It was fun, though,
because everyone was helping me do it.

Peter came over every day and worked just with me or
with me and Dad. He stopped going easy on me, and I
wanted to think it was because he didn't have to anymore.

Mike and Daniel even wanted to practice with me.
Mom wasn't too crazy about it when Mike and I would
stand at the top and bottom of the stairs, chucking the
ball back and forth, or when Daniel and I would dribble
it through the house, but she would only roll her eyes and
walk through, deftly stepping over the ball.

One day Dad even bought me my own pair of
cleats. Both of us made sure not to get all mushy about
it. But we both knew what it meant. I especially appreciated it because I knew money was so tight with Dad
out of work.

That night, I put Johnny's cleats under my bed and
tried on the new ones. They were a much better fit.

Johnny's hawk squawked from his cage. He seemed to
approve of the new shoes. I got up and gave him a treat,
noticing how big he'd grown. Soon he would be too big
for the cage. I didn't think he could fly yet. He only
hopped around when I let him out of the cage. But I had-
n't tested him lately. I made a note to myself to make time
to take him outside to see what he would do.

The next morning, I came in to breakfast dribbling the ball between my feet. I was in a good mood and eager to begin the day's practice session.

Everyone but Mom was already at the table. The first thing I noticed was that Mike and Daniel weren't fighting over who got to read the back of the cereal box, their usual routine. Instead, they were sitting there, eating without looking up.

I glanced at Dad to question what was going on, and he wore a similarly serious expression. I noticed he held an opened envelope in his hand. "What?" I asked, suddenly worried.

"It came today," Dad said, glancing at the letter in his hand. "They're not going to let you play."

"What? No…" I sputtered as I snapped the envelope away from him. Opening it, I scanned the writing. "How could they turn me down?" I cried indignantly.

"I got your hopes up," Dad said sadly. "I'm sorry. Grace, you're in great shape," he continued. "You can do something else. I talked to the girls' field hockey coach, and he said he'd be happy to have you try out."

Field hockey! Field hockey was fine, but it wasn't what I was training for.

Dad had already talked to the coach?

I flipped the envelope over and checked the postmark. This envelope had come a week ago! He'd already talked to the field hockey coach about me! I whirled around on Dad. "You never thought I was good enough! You never thought I could do it!"

I ran out of the house, furious. I wanted to talk to Peter, the only one left I could trust. When I got to his house, his mother told me he had gone to the rec center, so I headed there.

I found him shooting the soccer ball into the makeshift goals some guys had set up in the field. A little way off, Kate Dorset and her cheerleading crowd were practicing cheers. I noticed Jena was with them. Since when had she wanted to be a cheerleader? I supposed she needed new friends since I had more or less abandoned her for soccer practice.

"Hey," Peter said when he noticed me heading toward him.

"The board turned me down," I told him angrily. "My dad wants me to play field hockey. This is unbelievable!"

"Yeah, that stinks," he said dully. There was something in his voice that was off, as though he was only half paying attention to me.

He was looking over my shoulder. I turned to see Kyle pulling up in a car with his pals Joe, Craig, and Ben, all of them on the soccer team.

Kyle's glance darted my way for a second, but he made a conspicuous show of ignoring me. "Peter? You coming?" he called. "We only have the field for an hour."

Peter looked at me apologetically. "I've got to go."

"Yeah, you'd better," I sneered bitterly. So much for his being the one person I could count on. "I know you're still hoping Kyle's going to offer you a spot," I shouted after Peter as he headed toward Kyle's car. "I know you've only been training with me to improve your own game, right?"

He turned to say something to me, but then changed his mind and got into the backseat of Kyle's car. I had never felt more miserable and alone than I did right then. Everything had disappeared in a single morning.

As I trudged back across the field, Kate saw me and called out. "Hey, Gracie, want to go out for cheerleading? Oops! Sorry. Only girls can be cheerleaders." All around her, her friends laughed hysterically and no one laughed louder than Jena.

It wasn't my imagination. I truly did not have a friend in the world.

Fourteen

That night I lay on my bed, staring at the ceiling trying to make sense of everything that had happened. What had Dad thought he was doing all these weeks? What had he thought I was doing?

Was it a joke to him?

Deep down I knew it wasn't. He'd probably thought he was spending time with me even if it was all going to come to nothing in the end. It wasn't the worst thing a father could do, I supposed.

I wasn't ready to forgive him, though. He'd lied to me! He'd never believed in me at all!

I was so confused. Maybe what I wanted simply wasn't possible, and that was the reason girls didn't do it. Everyone on earth was aware of this but me, apparently. So what did that make me—some kind of idiot?

That had to be the answer. I was just plain stupid! I had believed that Dad had faith in me. I thought Peter was really my friend. I'd actually seriously thought that I could play on the boys' soccer team.

The only one who had been straight with me all along had been Mom. She told me that not everything is possible, but I thought she was the stupid one. I knew better. Well, ha-ha. The laugh was on me. Poor old deluded

Mom had known what was what after all. Girls just had to accept the crummy situation that was their lot in life.

With a light knock, Mom came into my room, holding the letter from the School Board. She might have been right, but I was in no mood to hear her tell me so. Turning away from her, I snapped, "Happy?"

She sat on a chair near my bed and didn't speak for a moment. "This isn't you," she said finally, "sitting here when you could be fighting back."

What? It wasn't what I'd expected her to say, not at all. I didn't know how to respond, so I didn't do anything, just lay there not moving.

"Soccer tryouts are Saturday," she went on. "Do you want to be there or not?"

Slowly, I rolled over toward her. "But you don't want me playing," I reminded her.

"No," she admitted, as though she was realizing it for the first time, "but this isn't my choice."

We looked at each other. Something big was happening between us but it was happening very quietly. She was saying that I could want something that she didn't want for me—and she would respect my choice. It was major and we both knew it. But we didn't know what to say or do about it.

Mom got up to leave, and then turned back. "Know what I wanted to be?" she asked.

"What?" I asked. It was odd to think of her as having ever wanted to be anything other than our mother or a nurse.

"A surgeon," Mom said.

"You?" I asked with a laugh of disbelief.

Mom laughed, too, but there was sadness in it. Not exactly sadness, more like longing. It made me immediately sorry I'd laughed at her because in that moment I could see it was something that still mattered to her, a disappointment that hadn't entirely gone away. She still wished she'd become a surgeon. How strange that I could know her all my life and not know something like that about her.

"Yes, me," she said, sitting back down. "So now I'm a nurse because it's as close as I could get."

What was she saying to me? I wasn't sure.

"If you want to limit yourself, fine," she said. "But don't let other people do it for you." She kissed my forehead and left me there to think about what she'd said.

*

There were wide steps and pillars in front of the Union City Board of Education building. It was imposing, to say the least.

I'd dressed neatly in the kind of outfit I'd wear to church. In my shoulder bag was the letter I'd received. It was signed from a person named C. Bowsher. It was C. Bowsher who had said I couldn't play on the boys' soccer team, and C. Bowsher was the one I now had to convince to change his mind.

I was terrified. C. Bowsher was only a person, but he was a grown-up, official person with the power to keep me from doing the thing I loved.

101

Taking a deep breath to steady my nerves, I headed up those big steps into the dark, quiet, solemn building. There were lots of closed doors and no one around to ask for directions. I felt as though I was walking through quiet halls for a long time, but finally I came to a door with the words "Chairman Bowsher" typed on a card next to the door.

When I opened the door, there were two secretaries dressed in suits at the desk. The older one stood behind the younger one reading something the younger one was typing. "Excuse me," I said, and my voice quivered. "I'm here to see C. Bowsher."

"You are?" the younger secretary inquired.

At that moment I knew I should have called to make an appointment, but I'd been scared that Chairman Bowsher wouldn't see me. I'd hoped that if I simply showed up, it would be harder to turn me away, that somehow I could make C. Bowsher listen to me. "I really need to see him," I pleaded.

"Her," the two secretaries corrected me at the same time.

My eyebrows shot up in surprise. It hadn't occurred to me that someone in such a high position could be a woman. The shocked look on my face must have been comical because both of them smiled.

"I'm Connie Bowsher," said the older of the two women, apparently not a secretary, as I'd assumed.

I didn't want to be overly optimistic, but this was an encouraging development. Instead of some stuffy old man in a suit, at least I'd be talking to a woman. As a woman in a powerful position, she must have had to face attitudes about a woman's limits all the time. *Unintentional slights like a teenaged girl assuming she must be a man,* I thought, embarrassed.

I took the letter from my bag and handed it to her. "Can we discuss this?" I asked.

Connie Bowsher invited me into her office. She listened intently while I told her how much soccer meant to me, how hard I'd trained, how I was sure I could play alongside the boys without a problem. "Sure" might not have been the entirely accurate word, but I was trying to be as persuasive as possible.

She wanted to know what had made me feel so strongly about soccer. I told her about my family's devotion to the game and Dad's college background. I hesitated a moment before telling her about Johnny's influence. It wasn't easy to speak to a stranger about something so personal, but she had a kind face and seemed genuinely interested.

We spoke for nearly an hour. She said I had convinced her, but she couldn't make a decision like this on her own. I would have to file an appeal with the School Board. "Our last meeting for the month is tomorrow," she told me, coming out from behind her desk and walking me to the door. "If you can get me an appeal before five, I'll present it to them."

I smiled till my face hurt. What luck that Mrs. Bowsher turned out to be such a nice woman!

"I can't promise you anything," she cautioned.

I told her that I understood and thanked her for her time. I nearly danced out of the building, feeling so hopeful. And not only hopeful but proud of myself that I hadn't simply accepted what the letter had to say.

My good mood disappeared as soon as I got outside and saw Dad standing at the bottom of the steps. He was not the person I wanted to see right then, when I was so elated by my accomplishment. Why did he have to come to ruin everything?

He misread my scowling face as I walked down the steps. "Couldn't change their minds?" he asked.

That's what he assumed, naturally! Gracie would once again fail!

I shook my head and delivered the shocking news: *I had actually accomplished what I came here to do.*

Almost.

Maybe.

"I have to file an appeal…by tomorrow," I said, without looking at him.

"Want help?" he offered.

"From you?" I scoffed. "No."

I had ridden my bike and now I stood at the rack unlocking it. Even though I wasn't looking at him, I could sense somehow that he was walking toward me. *What* did he want? I wished he would go away! I had nothing to say to him.

"Gracie," he began.

I wasn't ready to listen. Maybe I would never be. I swung my leg onto my bike and rode away, leaving him behind.

Fifteen

I sat at my desk writing, scratching out several thoughts, and then trying again with different words. This appeal had to be the best thing I had ever written in my entire life.

No.

It had to be the best thing the best writer in the world had ever written. And I wasn't the best writer in the world. In fact, writing wasn't something I was even that good at. I didn't have the patience for it.

But it was my last chance. Everything hung on this appeal. It had to be 100 percent convincing.

I tried to remember all the things I'd told Mrs. Bowsher, although I left out the part about Johnny. That wasn't something I was willing to share with some panel of strangers.

I had done some research in the library and learned something I hoped would support my argument. It was called Title IX and it had been made a law six years earlier, in 1972. I had written down its exact words: "No person in the United States shall, on the basis of sex, be excluded from participation in, be denied the benefits of, or be subjected to discrimination under any education program or activity receiving Federal financial assistance."

Although it didn't seem to be talking about sports specifically, I knew that the teams at Columbia High received money from the government and that had to count as federal funding. I decided to mention Title IX at the end of my appeal. I figured it never hurt to have the law on your side and, besides, it sounded cool and official, like I knew what I was talking about.

Something thumped against my bedroom window. It made the hawk squawk anxiously. "It's okay," I said, soothing him and feeding him a cracker as I leaned forward to check out the window.

Peter was under my window throwing his soccer ball up to get my attention. What did that traitor want? Not that I cared. I had no time for friends who weren't really friends.

Pulling down my shade, I turned from the window. It made me shudder to think that I had actually started liking Peter as more than a friend. He was nicer than Kyle, but he wasn't really all that different. He'd just been using me for his own selfish reasons.

I couldn't think about him for another second. He'd already wasted too much of the little time I had left to write this appeal.

The hawk made a funny little chirp and I looked at him. I remembered how I'd like to think that Johnny was in him. The idea had comforted me at the time, but now I didn't think so anymore.

Johnny wasn't inside the hawk. His spirit would never allow itself to be caged. Johnny was all around me. I could feel him when I played soccer and it was going well. It was as if I could hear his voice coaching me, believing in me, just as he had that day out on the rec center field when he'd believed I could kick that bottle off the post. With Johnny beside me, I'd done it.

Johnny had believed this hawk would fly again, and he'd believed I could play soccer against any boy. He'd bet five dollars that I could.

Sitting at my desk, I crumpled what I'd written before and started with a new idea. I decided I would tell the School Board about Johnny, after all. But I wouldn't talk about his death. I'd tell them about what I'd learned from him, both on the soccer field and off.

I began to write: *In many ways, I'm like the hawk with the broken wing that my brother Johnny rescued last summer.* Suddenly writing wasn't hard at all. Everything in my heart began to flow onto the page.

*

Mrs. Bowsher called right after her meeting to tell Mom that the Board had agreed to hold a hearing about my case. Dad came to my room to give me the news. I thanked him coolly. As soon as he left, though, I did a dance of joy all around the room.

Once I settled down, I reminded myself that there was still a long way to go. School Board meetings were held in the school auditorium. I had personally never been to one, but Mom had told me that they weren't that well attended. I sure hoped this one wouldn't be. I was nervous enough without the whole school staring at me.

Okay, I told myself, *take it one step at a time.* So far each step I'd taken had been a success. I could only hope the next one would be successful, too.

*

When I saw how well attended my particular School Board meeting was (during summer session, no less), it was pretty obvious that word had gotten out. The auditorium was packed with both students and parents. You would think I was asking to commit a federal crime instead of simply wanting to play a sport.

My whole family came. I wasn't exactly sure how I felt about that. I was still trying to avoid Dad, and my brothers weren't exactly on my list of favorites either. I now suspected they'd been in on the Gracie-can't-really-do-this-but-let's-make-her-feel-good aspect of my training. I knew, logically, that I couldn't really blame them. They meant well, but my feelings were still so hurt and I so resented their lack of faith that it was impossible to let my head rule my heart.

I was happy Mom came. At least I was sure one person there truly thought I should be fighting this.

The only other ally I was sure of was Mrs. Bowsher. She smiled warmly at me as I walked into the crowded auditorium and took a seat with my family in the front row. She sat at the center of a long table on the stage, flanked by six other School Board members, all men. A glance at them told me that they had copies of my appeal on the table in front of them.

108

There was a pretty impressive bunch of people who had come out to hear me make my appeal. Coach Colasanti was sitting onstage with the Board. So were Principal Enright and Mr. Clark. Coach Conners, the gym teacher who ran the girls' sports program at school, was also with them.

The members of the Varsity soccer team and their parents had come out. I figured they were there to object. Peter wasn't among them. I wondered if he had come over the other evening to warn me. If so, I was glad I hadn't spoken to him. Knowing they planned to be here would have made me sick with anxiety.

Kate Dorset and the entire cheerleading squad were there, too, including Jena, who I guess was planning on becoming a cheerleader in the fall. I couldn't imagine what reason they had to attend, except that wherever the soccer team went, they followed. Maybe they were there to protest the outrage of possibly having to cheer for another girl. What a concept!

Mrs. Bowsher called the meeting to order. I wasn't the only subject they had to talk about, but she put me first on the list and invited me to come to a table that was set up in front of the stage. A microphone had been set up, and I had to speak into it.

"Hello, my name is Grace Bowen and I am here to appeal a decision by the School Board ruling that I cannot play soccer on the boys' team because I am a girl," I began. I had never spoken into a microphone before, and at first I couldn't get used to the sound of my own voice booming in my ears. I realized I sounded higher than usual and quivery because I was nervous.

Once again, it was as though Johnny were beside me. I could almost hear him whisper in my ear: *See the target? Don't look at the target. Keep your eye on the ball.*

The target was the School Board. The ball was my appeal. And just as I had that day at the rec center, I needed to block out everything else around me and focus on delivering my appeal so that it would hit the target.

As I began reading the appeal, my voice grew increasingly steady. Even though the appeal was only two pages long, it felt as if it took forever to read. Then I came to the part I'd written about Title IX, and I knew I was almost to the end. "And finally," I read, "Title Nine, the federal mandate, requires equal access to sports for girls." I looked up at the Board. "Thank you."

Thunderous applause did not follow as I left the microphone and returned to my seat.

Mike, Daniel, Mom, and Dad clapped, though.

Otherwise, dead silence.

Mrs. Bowsher leaned into her microphone. "Coach Conners, tell us about Title Nine," she requested. "How does it apply here?"

"Title Nine means there is money to create a girls' soccer team," Coach Conners explained. "But there's no interest in creating one. You need more than one player to make a team."

That comment created a ripple of laughter from the cheerleaders and the soccer team. I forced myself not to look at them, as though they weren't even there.

One of the School Board members spoke next. "If another school in our district has a girls' team, does Miss Bowen have the option of playing there?"

"Yes," Coach Conners replied, "but no city in this state has a girls' soccer team."

"Why is that?" Connie Bowsher asked.

Coach Conners' tone of voice implied that the answer should be obvious. "It's not considered a girls' sport," she replied. "The girls I know would rather watch it than play it."

The soccer team and the cheerleaders thought this remark was just hilarious and let everyone know it.

Principal Enright spoke to the Board next. "We offer girls' gymnastics, field hockey, softball, tennis, swimming, badminton, track and field. All these teams could use a skilled athlete like Miss Bowen."

From the corner of my eye, I saw someone enter the auditorium. Turning, I realized it was Peter. He sat alone in the back aisle.

One of the Board members had a son on the soccer team. He said that the Board would like to hear from the team's captain to get their views on the subject. I figured that this was how word had gotten around.

Kyle smirked at me nastily as he sat where I had been, in front of the microphone facing the School Board. The cheerleaders burst into applause. "We on the team don't think Gracie Bowen should be playing with us," he began.

No surprises there. Would he have anything to add to that? Tensing, I waited to hear what he'd say next.

"Everyone will be afraid to play hard 'cause they'll be worried about her breaking something or whining 'cause she's bleeding," he went on.

What a reptile he was!

"She can't run as fast or kick as hard. I don't want to lose 'cause of her," he continued. He got up to go and then bent forward to the microphone for one last comment. "Just because she's Johnny's sister and he died, doesn't mean she should play."

I wondered if he said that last thing to provoke me into jumping out of my seat and punching him. The idea that he *wanted* me to try to kill him, or to act like a maniac in front of everyone, was the only thing that kept me seated.

Next, Mrs. Bowsher asked Coach Colasanti how many openings there would be on the soccer team. "I'll take the best two or three players who try out in the fall," he replied, speaking into his microphone.

"Define 'best,'" she requested.

"I look for speed, ball control, passing ability, toughness," he replied.

"All abilities a girl could demonstrate as well as a boy?" she asked.

"I've never seen it," he said.

"But, in theory, a girl might be able to possess these skills?" she pressed him.

Coach Colasanti wriggled uncomfortably in his chair, indicating that he was doubtful. "In *theory*, I suppose," he admitted dubiously.

A Board Member who hadn't spoken yet leaned forward. "If Miss Bowen were good enough to claim a spot on the team, why not let her play?" he questioned.

Once again, the coach squirmed in his seat. "There's the problem of the locker room. Showers. Changing into uniforms..."

"Thank you, Coach Colasanti, and everyone else for sharing your views," Mrs. Bowsher said, cutting him short and making it clear that the discussion was over. "The Board will take Miss Bowen's appeal under consideration and—"

"Wait!" Mom said, raising her hand and standing. "I'm Lindsay Bowen, Gracie's mother. I'd like to say something."

I looked up at her, surprised. What was she going to say?

"You have to be on the speaker's sheet in order to address this issue," Principal Enright objected.

Mrs. Bowsher wrote Mom's name on the sheet on the table in front of her. "There! Now she's on the sheet. Please, Mrs. Bowen, go ahead."

Mom walked up to the table with the microphone. Her voice shook more than mine had but she went ahead anyway. "All of you must be asking, if you were me, would I let my daughter play on a boys' team? Boys play hard. She could get hurt."

I didn't think Mom would let me down, but I wondered where this was going.

"I see her going out in the rain, in the dark. She won't give up," Mom went on. "She's fierce. She has a dream that's bigger and more important to her than any dream I've ever had."

She turned and looked at Dad, Mike, Daniel, and me for just a moment before speaking again. "For all my boys, soccer is and was everything. Gracie's the same. She loves competing. She loves that win-or-lose life." She faltered, as though considering her next words. "It's not the same for me. It's been lonely. She's my only daughter."

For some reason, my eyes went to Dad when she said that. Did he know how she felt? I hadn't realized she felt that way. He was watching her intently, almost as though he were seeing her for the first time.

"But no matter how I may have felt," she said. "I'd rather keep my loneliness than have her miss something she feels is so a part of her being."

Sixteen

My family and I sat in silence outside that auditorium on a hard bench for what seemed like forever. We were waiting while the Board discussed what they intended to do.

It was pretty clear that a lot of people didn't want me on that team, including Coach Colasanti. Obviously the fact that he liked me and my family personally didn't mean he thought he should have a girl on his team.

Eventually, Mrs. Bowsher came out of the auditorium to speak to us. I couldn't read her expression. It was completely businesslike. We all stood, looking at her expectantly.

"The Board split," she informed us. "I'm afraid I had to cast the final vote." She turned to me. "I have a daughter, too."

I wasn't sure what that meant.

Mom thought she knew and sighed. "We tried," she said in a defeated tone.

But Mrs. Bowsher grinned. "Don't be so quick to throw in the towel," she told Mom.

Dad's face lit up. "She gets to play?!" he asked. Did I see tears?

"To try out," Mrs. Bowsher clarified.

It took a minute for me to absorb this news. I wasn't definitely on the team, but I had taken a giant step closer to getting there. Step by step, I was winning!

"She'll make it," Dad assured Mrs. Bowsher as she turned and headed out of the school.

I almost smiled and hugged him, but I held back. He hadn't done this for me. I had done it for myself. If it had been up to him, I'd be playing field hockey in the fall.

I was happy, though. There was no denying it. I practically skipped to the school's double doors on my way out.

Outside, Peter stood by the door. I could tell from his hopeful expression that he was waiting to hear how it had gone. I wasn't about to tell him. Let him find out from his buddies on the soccer team. Without even a nod in his direction, I sailed on past him.

*

Soccer tryouts were in the first week of September, right before Labor Day. I was up early, dressed, and ready to ride my bike to school when Dad came out, offering to drive me there. I argued that I was fine on my own, but he insisted.

I knew he wanted to make things right between us. Part of me wanted to put the past behind us and forget about it. During the summer when we'd been training hard and I'd felt close to him, before I learned it had all been a lie, I'd been happy. Summer school hadn't even been that bad, since I knew that as soon as it was done for the day I could speed home on my bike and we'd work out together. It was over by the end of July, and then it was great having the entire day to practice with him.

But no matter how much I wanted to be friends with Dad again, I couldn't do it. I kept remembering how he'd let me down, and the anger would rise in me again.

I could see, though, that he wouldn't take no for an answer that morning, so I climbed into the backseat of the car. I waited to see if he'd insist that I get into the passenger seat beside him, but I suppose he decided it was enough that I was there at all.

On the ride to school, I attempted to give him the silent treatment. "So how are you feeling?" he asked, and I didn't reply. What was it to him how I felt? It was none of his business.

He realized I was ignoring him and dealt with it by doing all the talking the rest of the way. "The coach is going to make three cuts before lunch," he said. "He'll make three more cuts this afternoon and then more tonight. So pace yourself, blend in, be a team player."

Blend in? That made me laugh. "Like I'm not going to stick out or anything?" I said, forgetting to ignore him for the moment.

"Johnny once told me about this girl who hit a bottle off a fence, shooting barefoot from twenty yards." He tilted the rearview mirror my way to see me.

I turned away, not wanting to meet his eyes. I didn't know he knew about that. It shouldn't have surprised me that Johnny told him, though. That was Johnny—always wanting everyone around him to look as good as he did.

I opened the back door and got out. Dad rolled down his window. "I know you can do this," he said seriously.

Did he? It seemed as though he meant it. But I'd thought he'd meant it before and I'd been wrong. Still, as much as I wanted not to care about what he thought, I knew there was still part of me that wanted to prove to him that he'd been wrong.

With a quick nod, I headed across the field toward the school. Not only were there soccer tryouts today but there were also kids there to try out for track, football, and cheerleading. I tried not to pay attention to their stares and laughter as I walked past them to the soccer field, already crowded with a bunch of guys, all ready to try out.

Kyle and his little inner circle made sure to sneer at me as I approached. On the bleachers nearby sat some of their parents. They didn't bother to hide the fact that they were talking about me. A couple of them even pointed at me!

I saw Dad take a seat in the bleachers. I didn't know he'd planned to stay. *Forget about him,* I told myself as I began to stretch.

The tryouts began pretty soon after that. Coach Colasanti and Mr. Clark had us doing different drills…dribbling, passing, headers, and such. It was really fast-paced. I kept up with the others, but I wasn't outstanding or anything. That worried me. If I was going to get on the team, I'd have to be better than average. At least I was blending in—as best as I could hope to—as Dad had advised.

When it was time to practice free kicks, I more than held my own. It was one place where I was better than most. My kicks were definitely the most accurate, sailing into that sweet spot between the cone and the post.

After one particularly great kick, I saw Coach Colasanti conferring with Mr. Clark, and I could tell they were talking about me. They had noticed how good I was at free kicking. That had to be good news for me. Mr. Clark saw me watching and smiled. Coach Colasanti only wrote something on his clipboard and walked in the opposite direction.

At noon, the coach called a lunch break for an hour. Dad met me with a ham and cheese sandwich and a sports drink. We sat together in the bleachers while I ate. He nudged me when he saw Coach Colasanti step out of the school. "He's put up the list for first cuts," he said. "Go see."

It wasn't easy to make my way to the front of the crowd jostling to see the list posted on the board. It told who had been eliminated and who would go on for the afternoon tryouts.

I scanned the list of names of those who would continue. "B" should have been on the top, but it wasn't there.

And then I found it, scribbled in at the bottom, as though Coach Colasanti had meant to cut me at first but changed his mind at the last second.

Yes!

I'd won one more step!

Kyle was in the corner with his pals and saw my smile. He glared at me and so did the others. If I made the team, dealing with my teammates would be the toughest step of all, but I would worry about that later.

For the second set of tryouts that afternoon, we divided into teams and played a game. It was tough. Some of the guys were really good and they were giving it all they had.

More and more parents came to observe, and the bleachers were filling up. When I made a good play, some of them cheered for me, people I knew only slightly or not at all. It seemed that some people thought a girl should be allowed to play on a boys' team, and it felt good to hear them cheer. Of course, there were others who booed me. I did my best to pay no attention to them.

Mom arrived, sitting beside Dad to watch. And I noticed Jena sitting alone in the bleachers. I wondered if she'd been trying out for cheerleading.

I thought I was playing pretty well, though I felt very self-conscious. Guys came to block me, and it was as though they didn't know whether to be tough or back off. There was no time to stop and tell them to think of me as just another player. There were plenty of awkward moments.

The guys weren't the only ones who felt awkward, either. I was so much more aware of being a girl than I'd ever felt when I was practicing at home. I wanted to show that I was nice, not some kind of super-aggressive freak. I needed to prove I could be a team player, could fit in.

At one point I had the ball and was wide open to take a shot at the goal. "Shoot it!" Coach Colasanti bellowed from the sidelines.

Another player was nearby and he was dancing around, clearly wanting the ball. I saw the other team's players barreling toward me. In a second they'd be all over me, trying to take the ball. I remembered that day at the stadium how they'd ganged up on me and sent me sliding through the dirt.

In a moment of panic, I passed the ball to the open player who had been wanting it. With an impressive kick, he scored.

Nervous about what I'd done, I glanced at the coach. "When I say shoot, you shoot!" he yelled at me.

I knew that not listening to the coach would count as points against me. How much would it count?

It was on my mind as I waited near the trophy room for the second cut sheet to go up. When it did, I didn't wiggle my way up to the front like before. This time I waited, feeling pretty sure I'd blown it. I didn't want to give Kyle and his friends the satisfaction of seeing me get the bad news.

I waited until there was only one guy at the board. I could tell by the disappointment on his face that he'd been cut. I stepped forward, prepared to feel that same letdown.

But my name was there—right up with the B's where it belonged this time.

I leaped into the air, cheering.

I'd thought I was alone but Curt, Kyle's friend, passed by me from behind and bumped into me, sending me careening against the wall.

With the nastiest scowl, he walked out.

Dad came in and the smile returned to my face. "I made it!" I announced, too happy to be mad at him. He nodded but his face was serious. "What's wrong?" I asked as we walked side by side out of the trophy room.

"You passed because you didn't want to get hit," he said accusingly.

"Yeah, because they would have kicked my butt," I came back at him.

He stopped walking and looked straight at me. "Gracie, you've got to take it and you've got to give it. You've got to show them that you're no different."

It was hard to hear, but he was right and I knew it. If I was going to get on this team, it was what I had to do.

Seventeen

Union had one really great pizza place. Everybody went there. That evening my family grabbed a big round table and shared a pizza before I had to go back for the last round of tryouts.

It seemed that everyone else in Union who had tried out for any sport that day had the same idea. The place was jammed with familiar faces, not all of them friendly. It was nearly impossible for me to chew, knowing that so many people were either watching or talking about me.

I wasn't being paranoid, either. Just as some of them had done in the bleachers, some people—a few of them total strangers—barely made any effort to conceal the fact that they were talking about me. I felt that they wanted to see how I was holding up and read my expression to find out if I had made the last cut.

It wasn't all whispers and secret stares, of course. Some of my parents' friends stopped by the table and said "hi." They asked how it was going and wished me well. But other people we'd known for a long time from the neighborhood greeted us halfheartedly and kept going. It was as though my parents had committed some huge, embarrassing social blunder by allowing me to try out for the team. It was weird.

When I got up to use the bathroom, I had to walk right past the big table where a lot of the soccer team was eating. Kyle, Curt, Ben, Joe, Craig, and David just stared at me contemptuously as I passed them.

I supposed they were sure that with me on their team they would lose every game, and they blamed me for even attempting to play. But when I darted a sidelong glance at their angry, hate-filled faces, I had another thought. Assuming that wanting to win was what bothered them was probably giving them too much credit. It was more likely that they simply hated me for being a girl and daring to say that I could do whatever they could do.

The girls' room was quiet when I walked in. It was a welcome break from the clatter and loud voices in the restaurant. That was why I jumped when Jena, who must have been leaning against the bathroom wall, waiting, stepped out in front of me. "I saw you get up and so I came in here, too. I have to talk to you," she said.

I tried to get past her but she blocked me with her arm, placing her hand up against the wall. "I'm never going to understand why soccer is so important to you," she began. She seemed very uneasy, and I could see that this was hard for her. "But I'm sorry if I haven't been the greatest friend lately. I want us to be friends again."

I didn't know what to do. Hug her? Tell her it was okay that she'd mocked me along with the cheerleaders? "Kate Dorset might not like it if you were friends with me," I snapped, pushing past her.

"I'm not hanging out with Kate anymore," she said as she left the bathroom.

After Dad paid the bill (with money Mom passed to him under the table), we returned to the soccer field for the last round of tryouts. Late summer light still hung in the sky. People had come home from work by then and packed the bleachers to watch. Were tryouts *always* this crowded, I wondered, or was I the reason so many of them had come out?

My entire family was there now. Dad had even gone home and gotten Granddad. From the sidelines of the field, I saw Jena climb past the cheerleaders, who sat together in a group, and go farther up the stands to sit with my family. She waved to me and I returned the wave. I didn't feel angry at her anymore, not really. She had apologized and, after all, I had been the one who had suddenly become unavailable for our friendship because of my training. It was understandable that she'd been angry with me. I figured we were both to blame.

For this round of tryouts, we would play with the Varsity team. Everyone quieted down as the hopefuls walked onto the field along with the Varsity team. This would be, by far, the toughest part of the day.

Peter came out with the rest of the team. Neither one of us looked at the other.

Coach Colasanti divided us into teams and assigned our positions. When he blew the whistle, play began. It was only minutes before one of the players on the other side lost the ball and I was able to get hold of it. Almost immediately another player tried to get it away from me. He was a guy named Rodney who was also trying out. I knew him slightly from school. I had always thought he was a pretty good guy, but I didn't know what to expect now.

He made several attempts to get the ball from me, but I kept getting around him. Then he side-tackled me hard, slipping my legs out from beneath me. I went down hard on my side as the play went on without me.

From my spot on the ground, I saw Dad jump to his feet. "Hey! What was that?" he shouted angrily.

Coach Colasanti blew his whistle to stop the play, and I saw Mom gently pull Dad back down to his seat.

Rodney offered me a hand up, but I didn't take it. I couldn't tell if he was sincere or part of some Kyle-orchestrated plot to get me. I wouldn't put it past Kyle to turn even the other hopefuls against me. By offering his hand Rodney might just have been trying to cover up in front of the coach.

Coach Colasanti looked me in the eyes and then pointed to the loose ball, silently remarking on the fact that I had obviously failed to keep possession of it. He didn't seem pleased.

Later, the coach had the players stand shoulder to shoulder, ready to go one-on-one. It was just my luck to be paired with Kyle, of all people. "Whoever gets the ball first is offense," the coach said.

Kyle sneered at me. "Come and get it," he taunted nastily.

"My pleasure," I replied coldly, letting him know he wasn't getting to me.

The coach tossed the ball out about ten yards and then blew his whistle. Kyle and I both charged, but I was faster and got there first. Kyle was right behind me and steamrolled into me with his shoulder, knocking me down yet again and landing right on top.

"Get off of her!" This time it was Mom shouting angrily from the bleachers and Dad who had to pull her back down.

"The pleasure's mine," Kyle snickered as he got up.

I'd hit the ground on my elbow and it throbbed painfully. Coach Colasanti was at my side as I peeled myself slowly from the ground. "You all right?" he asked.

"I was wondering the same about your whistle," I grumbled, rubbing my arm. "Feel free to blow it at any time." *Couldn't he see what was happening?*

"You wanted to play with the boys," he remarked unsympathetically. They were going after me, and he was letting them.

The next thing we did was to go three on three for a shooting drill. I was with Rodney and another kid trying out named Oliver. We wore yellow pinnies. Once again, I was against Kyle! With him were Joe and Curt, in red.

"Listen up," Coach Colasanti said. "We're down to eight. Two of you will make the team."

I'd have to be better than six of these guys trying out, and it looked to me like they were all really good. I forced myself to put it out of my mind and concentrate on playing.

The coach tossed the ball and blew his whistle. I made up my mind to play as aggressively as I could. Curt was on me, in my face, all around. As I passed to Rodney, he whacked me in the shin with his cleats. "Sorry," he sneered, not one bit sorry.

Ignoring this new pain in my leg, I sprinted forward to get away from Curt. Rodney was being hounded by another player named Ben, so he passed the ball to me.

This was my chance to show what I could do, so I charged the goal. Joe came after me but I managed to stay ahead. When Ben saw what was happening, he left Rodney and joined Joe in trying to get the ball from me.

At the top of the box I ripped a bending ball into the upper corner of the goal!

SCORE!

Eighteen

The crowd cheered. I saw Peter smiling and even Mr. Clark was applauding, although he probably should have been more impartial.

The cheerleaders sat quietly with shocked expressions on their faces. That was even better than if they'd been clapping. I'd left them completely speechless.

My family and Jena, of course, went wild. Dad and Mom were both on their feet. "That's my girl!" Dad kept shouting over and over.

It felt so good!

Naturally, the Varsity team wasn't thrilled about it. Kyle stepped in front of me and spit on the ground. He shot his teammates a meaningful look and they nodded almost imperceptibly. The whole thing was so quick and small that no one else even saw it; Coach Colasanti certainly hadn't. But I saw, no doubt because I was meant to. They'd intended to scare me and they had succeeded.

Scared or not, I wasn't about to give up.

"Split into pairs," the coach instructed. "We're going to end with headers."

I was once again with Rodney. I'd decided that he was all right, not out to get me. Down the line, Peter was with another one of the kids trying out. Kyle was with a kid trying out named Mark.

Kyle suddenly turned to Rodney. "Mr. C. said to switch," he told him. "Work with someone new."

"I didn't hear him say that," Rodney objected.

"That's because you're a jerk," Kyle snarled. "Now move."

Rodney did as he was told and, though I couldn't blame him for not wanting to go against the captain of the team, I really wished he had stood his ground, because now I was paired with Kyle. We were face-to-face. For such a good-looking guy, he sure seemed ugly to me. "Be gentle with me," he said sarcastically.

"Go full-out for it," the coach told us as he tossed the ball into the air. Kyle and I both went up for it. I was closer and stretched forward to really snap it. Suddenly, Kyle elbowed me in the nose full force!

Again, I was on the ground. This time I couldn't get up. I was doubled over as blood gushed from my nose!

"Can't take the pain, don't play the game," Kyle said with an obnoxious snicker.

Blowing his whistle, Coach Colasanti rushed to my side. My family and Jena were on their feet, their faces filled with alarm. Rodney and Peter tried to help me to my feet, but I brushed them away and climbed to standing on my own.

"Bowen, you're out," Coach Colasanti said, pointing to the sidelines.

"To hell with you," I snapped at him, using my palm to stop the blood from streaming down my chin.

"What did she say?" the coach shouted indignantly.

"Good luck to all of you," Peter covered for me gamely.

"That's what I thought," he said to Peter, pretending to believe him. "Get lost before my hearing comes back," he told me gruffly.

*

Mom ran to the car for the first-aid kit. We stuffed gauze in my nostrils to stop the bleeding, and I held a cold pack on the bridge of my nose. Even though my nose hurt like crazy, she was pretty sure it wasn't broken because I wasn't getting black and blue under my eyes.

And then we waited, waited, and waited.

It felt like forever before Coach Colasanti posted the final list in the trophy room. But finally it went up.

My family and Jena hung back while I approached the bulletin board. Ahead of me, Rodney leaped in the air, hooting triumphantly. That meant there was only one other spot available.

And I didn't get it.

My name wasn't there.

I couldn't even look at my family. They only had to see my expression to know I hadn't made it. They had come to cheer for me but now there was nothing to say. I had let them down.

No, I hadn't.

I deserved to be on the team. Coach Colasanti had let them practically beat me up, all the while knowing he didn't intend to give me a fair chance.

Suddenly furious, I stormed past smirking Kyle and the rest of his idiot pals. Kate Dorset giggled as I passed.

"Grace!" Dad called after me, but I couldn't stop for him. I burst into the coach's office and found him doing paperwork. "I was good enough!" I shouted.

"That's why your name is there," he replied evenly.

What? "Where?" I asked, confused.

"Junior Varsity."

Junior Varsity? I hadn't even thought about Junior Varsity.

"If you're going to be the first girl on my team, you've got to be better than good," he said. "And you've got to act like you deserve to be there."

"I do deserve to be there," I insisted, and it felt good to say the words out loud.

He shook his head. "I hear it but I don't see it." He went back to his paperwork, letting me know that the discussion had ended.

"I offered your dad a part-time coaching job," he told me when I was nearly out the door.

I knew that was good news, but it didn't make me feel any better. Dad was in, but I wasn't!

*

That night, Dad went right upstairs, showered, and came down again dressed in his uniform for work. Somehow, he'd gotten his old job back. "My supervisor called to tell me that he put my absence down as unpaid leave. I'm in the warehouse again and I have to work the late shift, but it's a job."

"And after work you get to coach," I said coldly. "Glad it all worked out for you."

It was so unfair! I went into the backyard, letting the door slam behind me. Pulling off my cleats, I tossed them into the darkness, never wanting to see them again. I'd won at every step except the one that counted, the last one.

Dad came out the back door into the yard. "You know, Gracie, I'm not crazy about working this shift, but sometimes you have to take what you're offered and make the best of it," he said.

"Not me," I said firmly. "I'm quitting."

Dad sighed deeply. "Johnny was a star but—"

I put my hand up abruptly to stop him. "I don't want to hear about Johnny," I snapped.

"He played more for me than for himself," Dad pressed on anyway. "You're different. You truly love the game. You play for yourself, and that gives you a drive and toughness that's more important than size and speed."

"That's coaching crap," I scoffed, turning away from him.

"Grace, quit if you want!" he cried, starting to get angry. "But quit because you're not good enough! Quit because you'll never be good enough! Don't quit because you got your feelings hurt. You've got to dig deep and come out as strong and tough as anyone."

"I did!" I cried.

"No!" he disagreed. "I know what you can do, but it's not enough for me to believe in you. You've got to make them *all* believe in you!"

We stood there staring at each other. Then he turned and headed toward the house.

"How do I do that?" I yelled at his back, desperate to know the answer. I'd done everything I could think of. If there was something more, he had to tell me, because I had no idea what it could be.

He turned around to me. "You *know* what to do," he said before going in.

My head fell forward in despair. I didn't know.

My nose throbbed and ached all along both cheekbones. My cleat-scraped shins screamed with pain. My hip and arms were bruised and burning.

It occurred to me very slowly as I stood there with my head hung in defeat and my body aching that it was possible I had miscounted the steps.

Maybe I *hadn't* failed at the last step because I hadn't come to the last step yet. These tryouts were simply *another* step toward my dream, not the final one. And if that was really the case, then I hadn't failed. I had *succeeded* in advancing to the next step, which was to play soccer on the boys' Junior Varsity team.

Nineteen

Junior Varsity soccer was definitely the B team. Even the field was second-rate, bumpy and weedy compared to the perfectly manicured Varsity field.

When I arrived for our first practice, the freshmen and sophomores on the team stared at me as though I were a creature from outer space. At least I wouldn't have to worry about them being much bigger than me. Without making any reference to me, Mr. Clark, who coached the team, simply blew his whistle for practice to begin.

I appreciated that he didn't make a big fuss. And, deep down, I also enjoyed the way he kept smiling at me, as if he completely approved of my being on his team and was even proud of me. After facing down so much negative attention, it was a refreshing change.

Another refreshing change was not being mowed down by hostile, fire-breathing opponents bent on my destruction. The guys on the JV team were good players, but they weren't as big and aggressive. Without Kyle in the lead, they weren't overwhelmed with resentment at the mere thought of my presence.

After practice ended each day, I stayed on to practice kicking on my own. It had always been what I did best, so I figured I should play to my strength and become really excellent at it. It was the most direct route I could think of to become an invaluable player on the team. If I could be an outstanding player on JV, I could win a spot on the Varsity team.

It was often dark before I stopped firing balls at the goal. I stayed at school to practice because the field was bigger than my yard and the goalpost itself was exactly where it would be during a real game. I could blast balls into the goal from different spots on the field, too.

One night, someone pulled up to the parking lot and watched me practice from the car. Squinting over the glare of his headlights, I saw Coach Colasanti watching me from behind his steering wheel.

Ignoring him, I blasted a ball into the upper-right-hand corner. I knew he saw it. I was hoping he was regretting his decision not to let me play Varsity.

Another evening, just as the last of the light was dying out, Peter showed up carrying a white bag from a deli nearby. He stood on the sidelines, apparently wanting to talk to me. I just ignored him and kept practicing.

"Kyle didn't want me on the team," he called to me. "He wanted to practice with me to improve his game."

I know how that feels, I thought bitterly. I was glad to hear that he'd gotten a taste of his own medicine, as the saying goes. Did he want me to feel sorry for him after he'd done the exact same thing to me? I kept kicking balls into the goal, pretending he wasn't there.

I could feel Peter watching me. Finally I couldn't resist taking a quick peek at him. The stricken expression on his face made me miss my kick. "Johnny…he left me, too," he said in a voice choked with emotion. He brushed his eyes quickly. He was crying!

That stopped me altogether. I had been so wrapped up in my own grief that I'd never stopped to consider how Johnny's death had affected Peter. But I should have. Johnny was his best friend.

He walked out between the goalposts. I shot one to him and he caught it. "Anyway," he said. "I have a best friend again. And I'm going to stay here with her until she's done."

He handed me the white bag. There was a ham sandwich and a soda inside. He'd brought it for me.

I ate the sandwich there on the field and then went back to practicing. Peter took out a flashlight and a book. He sat on the sidelines reading while I practiced.

I couldn't stay angry at him. He'd only wanted what I had wanted…to play Varsity soccer. And so what if he wanted to practice with me to improve his game? That had been why I wanted to practice with him.

Practicing felt a lot less lonely with Peter sitting there waiting. I was glad he came.

*

Once school was in full swing, there was more than just soccer in my life once again. I knew that I couldn't stay on the team if I failed anything, so that was all the incentive I needed to keep my grades up. Besides, school seemed less dull than it had the year before. Somehow I had found my way back to caring about my classes again.

One afternoon I had some time after school before practice began. Instead of going home, I went to the library to study for my big chemistry test the next day. I was at a table with a thick textbook in front of me when I sensed that someone had taken a seat across from me and was staring a hole through the book. "Heard that's a good book," Coach Colasanti said.

I held up the cover to show him that it was my chemistry text. "Want to borrow it?" I joked dryly.

After that he got right to the point of his visit. "We drew Kingston as our first game. The whole town is coming out. I want you there."

I lowered my book and tried not to let my jaw drop at the same time. "To play?" I asked cautiously, not sure I understood but hoping it was what he was saying.

"To support your team," he said.

I should have known, I thought, fighting my disappointment. "You mean sit on the bench," I said.

He grimaced slightly and nodded. It was exactly what he'd meant.

He slid a black band across the table to me. "The team's wearing armbands for Johnny," he explained. Instantly, a lump formed in my throat. In that case, I would definitely be there.

That evening, after practice and my extra kicking session, Peter drove me home. I told him about the armbands. He already had one. We agreed that even though the night would bring up a lot of emotion for both of us, we thought it was a good way to honor Johnny's memory.

Later, alone in my room, I noticed that the hawk seemed restless, banging around his cage. I wondered if his cage was too small now. Maybe he didn't even need a cage anymore. His wing should have been mended by now.

It was time to find out.

Everyone in the house was busy. Mom was doing laundry. Mike and Daniel were watching *The Brady Bunch* on TV. Dad was working the night shift. No one noticed as I left the house with the hawk in his cage.

Outside, I put him in the basket of my bike and rode to school. The night lights were on, making it possible for me to see way out onto the soccer field. I climbed up the bleachers to the top row. I set the cage down and opened the door.

Part of me hoped he wouldn't come out, but a larger part knew I had to see if he could fly. "Come on. It's okay," I coaxed him. I extended my hand into the cage, letting him hop on. Carefully, I drew him out.

He blinked in the bright lights, confused. Slowly, he hopped up my sleeve. I moved my arm, hoping the motion would startle him into flying. He only held on, digging his talons into my jacket. "Go on!" I told him. "It's better out there."

The hawk turned his head to me and blinked. He didn't want to go, and I didn't really want him to go, either.

Then why was I doing this?

Because I knew it was right for him. He couldn't stay in a cage forever. He was a wild bird—powerful, a hunter,

139

meant to soar in the sky. As long as he stayed in that cage, he could never experience the life he was born to live.

All at once, the hawk spread his wide wings. With a flurry of moving feathers, he rose into the air.

Tears stung my cheeks as he disappeared into the dark sky. He had been my confidant all through these long, hard months. Often, he was the only one I could talk to. He reminded me of Johnny, a loyal friend I could count on.

But, I suppose, when loved ones move on, you can't stop them. You can only hold them in your heart, never forgetting what they meant in your life. And, in that special way, the ones you love never really leave.

Twenty

On the night of the Columbia/Kingston game, the soccer stadium was electric with excitement. The lights were turned on to full wattage. Beneath their white-hot glare, the school band pounded out a fight song. The cheerleaders pulled out all their best moves, cheering at top volume as they formed towering pyramids.

I was running late, probably because I'd taken my time at supper, procrastinating, not really sure I wanted to be there. For Johnny's sake, I wanted to attend. I was all for showing school spirit, but sitting with the Varsity team would be more than a little weird, knowing how they felt about me.

When I finally got there, everyone had left the locker room already. Only Mr. Clark was still there. He smiled as I hurried in and he took a uniform wrapped in plastic from a cardboard box. It was a Varsity uniform. He ripped open the plastic, handing it to me. "Grace, they told me to give you this," he said.

I wasn't sure how I felt. I was going to put on a Varsity uniform, just for this one night. It should have been a dream come true, but instead it was confusing. Somehow it felt wrong to put it on and not really be on the team. "I know I'm not playing," I told him.

"I have something else for you," he said, reaching into his own gym bag. "Last season, after the big game, I found Johnny's jersey." It was Johnny's, all right, washed but well-worn Number 7.

"They retired this number," I reminded him, taking the jersey and holding it close to my chest.

"I think Johnny would want you to wear it," he replied. "Coach C. said it would be all right. The number belongs to your family now. I've been keeping the jersey for you."

I ran my hand along the smooth cloth, feeling so touched. Mr. Clark had kept it, sure that someday I would be worthy of it. It meant a lot to me to have the jersey, and it made me happy that he'd had so much confidence in me all along.

I thanked him and went to the girls' locker room to put on the uniform with the Number 7 jersey. Studying my image in the mirror was a strange experience. What did it mean that I was wearing this uniform, this number? I wasn't sure.

Before I went out, I took one last item from my gym bag: the black armband for Johnny. The tears that filled my eyes as I slipped it onto my arm surprised me. I'd thought I was past that, but maybe I would never be beyond tears when I thought of Johnny's death. It was possible that I didn't even want to put that stage behind me if it meant I had to forget him, even a little bit.

Heading out to the field, I saw the Columbia Cougars warming up, some kicking free shots, others heading balls in a circle. They were practicing, but they were also showing off for the fans, getting the crowd psyched. All of them, including the two newest players who had beat me in tryouts, wore black armbands for Johnny.

With my eyes on the players out in the field, I made my way to the bench to sit with the other second-stringers. Principal Enright glowered at me as I passed. I could tell he wondered what I was doing there. From the corner of my eye, I saw him gesture to Coach Colasanti. I had the feeling he was going to demand that I leave.

The coach was over on the sidelines, talking to Mr. Clark. His eyes darted to Principal Enright and then to me, sizing up the situation. Then he turned back to Mr. Clark, as though he hadn't noticed us, although I knew he had.

Peter was already seated on the far end of the bench when I got there. He leaned forward and waved to me. Noticing the Number 7 jersey, he nodded with approval. It helped me feel less like an outsider knowing that he was there and that he was okay with my wearing Johnny's jersey. He beckoned to me to come sit beside him, which I did.

I was the only player from JV who was on the bench, although I had spotted almost all the other JV players in the bleachers, also wearing the armbands. Some waved and gave me a thumbs-up sign.

My family climbed into the stands, Dad carrying Granddad up. Jena was with them and she waved to me. I waved back.

143

The crowd quieted as the Kingston Gladiators jogged double-file out onto the field. They wore their sweats with the hood up, hiding their faces. Their sweatshirts had STATE CHAMPS emblazoned across the front, just in case we might have forgotten the fact, as if that were possible. They chanted a warlike grunting song meant to intimidate the Cougars and their fans. To be perfectly honest, they *were* big, tough, and scary-looking.

As soon as the whistle blew, the game went into full swing. I'd never seen players hit each other so hard or run so fast. Ben from the Cougars got slammed almost instantly by a Kingston player. When another Kingston player shot, Craig made an amazing save. He passed to Curt, who set up the ball for Kyle, allowing him to race in to score for Columbia.

The Columbia fans cheered wildly.

Kingston's huge secret weapon, The Giant, made the next goal, sending the ball sailing past Ben, Joe, Craig, Curt, and Kyle. The five of them looked stunned, like they'd never seen a ball traveling at that speed. The Giant was even more powerful than he had been the year before. He was not going to be easy to get around.

Late in the second half, the score was 3–3, with less than five minutes remaining on the clock.

Just at that moment, a Kingston player plowed into Ben feet first, gouging his leg with his cleats. Coach Colasanti put Peter in as Ben came limping off the field. I smiled at Peter, happy for him that he would get to play.

The game was going down to the wire. Whoever scored next would probably win.

And then one of the Kingston players made a really obvious foul on Kyle. He elbowed him in the stomach as he ran by, and Kyle went down.

The crowd jumped to its feet even before the ref blew his whistle a second later.

The coach called Peter over and quickly said something to him. In a few seconds Peter ran right over to Kyle, who was struggling to get back up. Whatever it was Peter said to him, Kyle was clearly not happy about it. He seemed to be arguing with Peter.

Peter kept his hand on Kyle's shoulder. To someone who didn't know the two of them, it might have looked as though Peter was checking to see if Kyle was all right. But I *did* know them, and I felt fairly certain that the coach had told Peter to make sure Kyle didn't get back up. In fact, I was positive that was what was going on when, in the next moment, Coach Colasanti called for an injury substitution. The coach was strategizing something, though I wasn't sure what he had in mind.

I glanced down the bench, wondering who he'd call. All the second-stringers were leaning forward eagerly.

Peter tried to help Kyle off the field, but Kyle brushed him off as he approached the coach. "Mr. C., I'm fine," he insisted. "I can stay in."

"I'm making a change," the coach told him brusquely. He turned to the bench, ignoring the red-faced, furious Kyle. "Bowen," he called.

I heard him say my name, but it was as though he had spoken it in a language I didn't understand. My mind couldn't make sense of why he was saying my name. I just sat there.

"Bowen!" he shouted, this time impatiently.

That's when I snapped to attention, still not certain what was happening. I approached Coach Colasanti as he strode over to me. "Get in there," he ordered. "I want you to take the free kick. Can you do it?"

The answer was yes, of course. I had to say "yes" and I had to believe that was the true answer.

With a nod, he indicated that I should get out onto the field. "Whatever you do, hit the target!" he shouted from behind me, and then instructed Joe to drop back to the middle.

As I continued making my way onto the field, a mix of boos and cheers came from the stands. The sound of my family cheering themselves hoarse came through loud and clear. I also thought I heard Jena let out a high-pitched cheer.

"What are you doing?" Curt snarled when I reached the other players.

"Taking the shot," I informed him in a matter-of-fact tone.

"You've got to be kidding me!" he cried angrily. "Oh man, this had better be good."

Peter smiled at me. "You can do it, Gracie."

"Don't blow it," Craig growled.

I took two steps back and eyed the goal. I steadied myself and tried to relax. Then I sprang forward, charging the ball, and kicked.

The ball was in the air.

There was nothing left to do but watch it sail forward.

The Kingston goalie dived for it. He stretched up, but the ball was too high for him to reach.

It was headed right for the net…and then…it bounced off the post!

I had missed!

Inside I just caved with shame and disappointment. All around, my teammates kicked the ground or spit angrily.

I heard Coach Colasanti's voice, and I was sure he would call me out of the game. "Move! Move! Move!" he shouted to me.

"Move where?" I shouted back.

"Follow the ball!" he cried. "You're playing forward."

I knew I had to play as if it was the only chance I would ever have to play Varsity soccer, maybe the last opportunity to ever play soccer again!

Peter and the other players were setting up for a corner kick. Curt ran along beside me. "I'm going near. You swing around the back post," he instructed on the run.

I nodded.

"You'd better be there," he added before peeling away.

The Gladiators intercepted the ball before it got to the back post, but in that moment something changed. My teammates started working with me, including me in plays, no longer shoving me around or trying to make me look bad. And that allowed me to forget about myself or what I had to prove. I could just focus on the ball and the plays.

I felt as though I were flying up and down the field. My head was completely there…nowhere else, able to ebb and flow along with my team. Everyone was working together and so we made great shots, perfect passes, and unbelievable saves.

After our goalie, Craig, made one of those amazing saves, he had two choices. He could pass it to one of our fullbacks or to me. I was closer to the goal, the obvious choice.

He hesitated a split second…and then passed the ball to me.

I worked the ball up the wing, my feet flying. The Gladiators were on me immediately.

I needed to pass the ball off a couple of times in order to avoid having it stolen, but I got it back each time and was soon at midfield.

Just when I thought I was clear for a shot, a Kingston Gladiator side-tackled me, slamming me to the ground as the ball rolled out of bounds. A loud moan of sympathy came from the Columbia Cougar fans.

In seconds I was up and poised to take the throw-in, but I didn't get the chance. The Cougars lost the ball, but I thought I saw a chance to get it back. Swooping in front of the Gladiator, I dived in and stole the ball!

The crowd was on its feet. Coach Colasanti and Mr. Clark were both shouting something that I couldn't hear as I raced toward the goal.

Then something happened I never would have believed. The cheerleaders were chanting my name! "Grace! Grace! Grace! Grace!" They were cheering for me!

A Kingston player ran in to tackle me. For the fastest second, the film of Pelé that Dad had played for me flashed into my mind.

I took the hit as he slammed into me, knocking me back. But I forgot the painful shock and concentrated on absorbing his energy, making his weight and speed work against him. Bouncing back from the ground, I saw his moment of hesitation, and in that moment I stole the ball back.

Dimly aware that the crowd was on its feet roaring, I moved the ball down the field. There was nothing around me now, not a sound, not another player, not the coach, not Dad.

There were only Kingston players to be avoided, gotten around, outrun. I moved the ball this way and that...cut, cut, cut.

Curt was ahead of me, open to make the goal. I was about to push the ball to him, but saw Kingston players peeling off in his direction. A Kingston player rushed toward me. I faked as if I were going to go around him. His balance shifted. His legs were wide. I slid the ball between his legs...ran past him. Now it was just the goalie and me. *Be with me, Johnny, be with me.*

I saw the goalie crouch, lean to one side. He gave me some net. Another Kingston defender rushed toward me. I could see his huge legs sliding toward me. Now! I had to do it now! The crowd excitement was deafening. I heard Coach C. yell: "Shoot! Shoot! Shoot!"...and then I struck it perfectly with my instep. The ball sailed toward the goal. It was surreal. I watched the goalie, arms fully outstretched, dive…the ball near his fingertips…sure that once again, I'd be denied. *Please, just this one time…* and there it was. It was past him crashing into the lower corner of the net. GOAL! Golden Goal! COLUMBIA WINS!

I dropped to my knees.

The Columbia fans erupted with wild screams of joy. They were in a frenzy, jumping, hooting, and hugging each other. They streamed onto the field, embracing the players, lifting them high. They were rushing toward me.

There was only one person I wanted to share this moment with. I looked up to the bleachers. "Dad?" I called. "Daddy?"

Where was he?

And then suddenly he was there beside me. He hugged me tight, lifting me off my feet. "You did it!" he cried. "You did it!"

I nodded, hugging him as tears streamed down my face. *Yes! I did it!*

I did it for the team, did it for Dad. I did it for Johnny. Deep down inside, I knew that I had done something special for myself that would change me. This was an amazing moment, a personal victory. I knew that Johnny's memory would be kept alive…forever…in the lives of all those he touched.

As he believed in me, I believe him…*I can do anything!*

The True Story of *Gracie:*
With an Afterword by Elisabeth Shue

Gracie *is a work of fiction. The characters and events are made up. But this story has its basis in real-life events that took place in the lives of the Shue family, who lived in Maplewood, New Jersey. One of the chief inspirations for the film was Elisabeth Shue. In* Gracie, *Elisabeth, an Oscar-nominated actress with many films to her credit (most recently* Dreamer *with Dakota Fanning), plays Gracie's mother, Lindsay Bowen.*

Like Gracie, Elisabeth grew up in a family with three brothers, all of whom loved and played soccer, as did their father. In real life, she was the first girl at her school to play soccer on the boys' team. The afterword by Elisabeth Shue that follows describes her memories of that momentous day.

Afterword

I was in the sixth grade. My eighth-grade brother, Will, had taught me how to play soccer. I wanted to follow his example. Tryouts for a boys' team at Cameron Field in South Orange, New Jersey, were being held on a Saturday morning. My dad and I talked about whether I wanted to try out. I remember how nervous I felt when I decided to do it.

When we arrived, there were about eighteen boys dribbling and passing. Coach Gene Chyzowych had given each boy a ball. I swallowed hard, ran onto the field, and said hello to the coach. He gave me a ball, too. I felt very exposed and hoped none of the boys could see me shaking. I began to dribble, just as Will and my younger brothers, Andrew and John, and I did at home in our yard.

In less than minute, an older boy from our neighborhood ran at me, kicked my ball away, and taunted: "Girls can't play." That did it. I burst into tears and ran off the field to the sideline, where my dad was watching.

"What's wrong?" Dad asked.

"A boy took the ball from me. I want to go home."

My dad took my hand and practically dragged me back onto the field, saying: "We're not going home!" Then he interrupted Coach Chyzowych and told him what had happened.

Mr. "C.," as he was called, blew his whistle. "Boys," he said, "come over here, please."

Now I was a spectacle. All the attention was on me. I didn't know what would happen next. With all the boys gathered around and quiet, he said, in his native Ukrainian accent, some of the most validating words I'd ever heard: "Boys, soccer is a game for boys *and* girls. Lisa Shue has just as much right to a ball as each of you." He had been holding a ball as he talked, but then he put it on the ground and passed it to me. Thank goodness, a couple of boys came up to me and we began to pass to each other.

That moment in 1975 was a turning point in my life. I often think how similar moments must have been happening all over the country, and how so many other girls, like me, must have felt anxious but managed to find the courage to prove that they belonged on the field with boys.

Thank you, Mr. C.

With love from your first girl player, Elisabeth Shue.

When Elisabeth hit high school in ninth grade, the school wouldn't let her play on the boys' team anymore. Unlike Gracie, Elisabeth shifted her attention and athletic ability over to gymnastics.

Elisabeth began to appear in commercials and then movies. She also went on to college, first Wellesley and then Harvard, where she continued her interest in sports, playing field hockey and, later, soccer. By the time she got to Harvard women's soccer teams had come into being, and Elisabeth was able to play on the Harvard women's team.

Meet Carly Schroeder, the Young Star of *Gracie*

"My soccer boys are the *best!* I had so much fun with these guys. They played in the rain, heat, cold temps, and all night when they had to. They were so inspiring because of their passion for the game. I had the best time on this movie," says Carly Schroeder, the young actress who plays Gracie Bowen.

Carly is young (she turned sixteen on October 18, 2006), but she's already been working as an actress for ten years. She started as a child on TV playing Serena Baldwin on the long-running daytime drama *General Hospital* and also on its sister show, *Port Charles*.

Leaving daytime behind, Carly moved on to something completely different—comedy. She played Melina Bianco, Matt McGuire's devilish best friend, on the Disney channel's popular *Lizzie McGuire* and also in *The Lizzie McGuire Movie*. She has lent her voice to two movies—*Babe: Pig in the City* and *Toy Story 2*—and also models, recently for Abercrombie & Fitch and Jessica McClintock.

On the big screen, she played Cindy Brady in the movie *Growing Up Brady*. She has appeared in several independent films, including *Mean Creek*, *Prey*, and *Eye of the Dolphin*, as well as in *Firewall*, with Harrison Ford and Virginia Madsen. She's proud of all these movies, but working on *Gracie* will always be special to her. It was an experience she calls "unforgettable."

She told fans: "The Shues have renamed me Carly Shue because I am part of their family now. I wear that title proudly. I have never put so much energy into a movie. Each day, I was either physically challenged by soccer or my day was filled with emotional scenes. This movie and Davis Guggenheim [the director and husband of Elisabeth Shue] have made me a better actress because Davis went for specific details, and we connected artistically. This was a story about his wife and her family, so he could express exactly what he needed in each scene."

Carly was not a soccer player when she was first cast in the role of Gracie, but she is very athletic. In her free time she enjoys horseback riding, fencing, karate, scuba diving, and surfing. She worked extremely hard to add soccer to her list of athletic achievements and accomplished that goal in a short time.

To learn fast, she trained at Catz Sports in Pasadena, California. (Carly lives with her family in Los Angeles, but she's originally from Valparaiso, Indiana.) "I have to play against large boys in the movie," she told fans, "so they wanted to make sure I was physically fit to take the beatings."

In addition to weight training and workouts with the regular trainers at Catz, she also worked with Dan Calichman, who used to play for the Los Angeles Galaxy professional team. She says she learned a lot from him: "The man has skills."

The training wasn't easy, but Carly felt she got the best possible result by working at Catz Sports. She says: "If you are in sports and you hope to hit your highest potential, then you should train here. The results are amazing."

Carly got to meet some of the great women soccer players of our time: Mia Hamm, Kristine Lilly, and Abby Wambach, while working on a DVD for soccer that aims at helping kids improve their game. "These three girls are incredible people," she says. "They love what they are doing, and they are thankful every day to be playing the game."

In April 2007, when Carly got her driver's license and a car, she and her mom took a road trip together so Carly could gain the confidence she needs behind the wheel. She told fans: "It was an awesome (white knuckles at times) good time. Mom made me drive for two hours through the mountains above Ojai. I was so afraid I was going to wreck my new car. I checked out a college in upper California, but I think it is too far from LA to work with my acting career."

You can write to Carly at:
1560 Newbury Rd., Suite # 167, Newbury Park, CA 91320

What Is Title IX?

In *Gracie*, the character of Gracie Bowen appears before the Board of Education to petition their decision not to let her play soccer on the boys' team. One of the things she does is read Title IX to them. What is it?

Gracie used Title IX to bolster her case because in 1978, when the story takes place, girls' soccer teams did not exist in most schools. Barely 10,000 girls in the whole country played soccer in high school, and these were usually intramural and pickup games, not formal teams. But things were changing.

In 1972, Congresswoman Patsy Mink was assisted by Congresswoman Edith Green in writing an act that came to be known as Title IX. Now known as the Patsy T. Mink Equal Opportunity in Education Act, Title IX of the Education Amendments of 1972 stated: "No person in the United States shall, on the basis of sex, be excluded from participation in, be denied the benefits of, or be subjected to discrimination under any education program or activity receiving Federal financial assistance."

Although Title IX did not apply only to girls' sports, that's where it had its greatest impact. Since almost all public schools received money from the federal government in Washington, D.C., the schools had to comply with the act or lose their government money. Complying meant that as much money had to be spent on girls' sports as on boys' sports. It also meant that girls had to receive equal access to sports competition.

Nonetheless, Title IX was simply ignored by many school districts, in some cases because they simply did not know about it. The districts would be able to go on as they always had until someone like Gracie Bowen challenged them for not complying with the ruling.

At the same time in the 1970s that Title IX was becoming increasingly well known and acted upon, the women's liberation movement was also growing. Women who were known as feminists challenged society's ideas about the role of women. They held rallies across the country to demand equality in all areas of life.

In 1972, the same year Title IX was passed, the Senate, responding to the growing women's movement, voted 84 to 8 to send the Equal Rights Amendment to the state legislatures to vote on. The Equal Rights Amendment, also known as the ERA, stated simply that: "Equality of rights under the law shall not be denied or abridged by the United States or by any State on account of sex."

By 1982, which was the deadline for passing this amendment, it did not have enough votes to pass. In 1993, a Congressional bill to revisit the ERA vote also failed.

Nonetheless, things have changed for women.

As a result of Title IX, dozens of colleges across the country have established Varsity soccer teams. By 1981 there were over 100 Varsity teams established in NCAA women's soccer and even more club teams.

At the same time that women's participation in sports was growing, the popularity of soccer for both males and females was also rising. For many years, soccer had been less popular in the United States than it had been in the rest of the world. But by 1980, almost 900,000 young people were playing soccer on teams, and more than half of the players were female. That number has continued to grow.

In 1985, the first women's National Squad was formed. These players received little attention from the public or the press. With a lack of attention, the squad broke up for periods of time and suffered from inconsistent training.

In 1991 the establishment of the Women's World Cup changed all that. The tournament was held in China in 1991, and it would give the U.S. women's team a chance to prove what they could do. It introduced the world to soccer players Mia Hamm, Michelle Akers, Brandi Chastain, Julie Foudy, and others who would be stars of the sport for the next decade. Each of their games was attended by nearly 200,000 people. The hard-fought tournament resulted in a victory for the U.S. team. Although this victory received little notice in the U.S., those in the soccer community knew that a new era of women's soccer had arrived.

In the coming years, the women's professional soccer team enjoyed a growing advantage over the teams in other nations, thanks to Title IX. It could pick from an enormous pool of talent coming out of the nation's colleges, girls who had been playing from a young age.

The year 1996 was a landmark for women's soccer. That year women's soccer was added to the lineup of the Olympics. NBC gave no coverage to the women's events, but the crowds in the stands grew with every game. In the end, the U.S. took home the gold!

In 1999, the World Cup was held in Pasadena, California. Things had changed since 1991. The turnout in the stands was huge. Even Bill Clinton, who was president of the United States at the time, was there. In the last round the U.S. played against the Chinese women's team. The teams seemed equally matched. In the end, the game went into penalty kicks. American goaltender Brandi Chastain made the fifth kick, winning the game.

The crowd in the stands went wild with joy. "I think the whole country was caught up in this," said President Clinton, "not only fans of soccer but young girls, too. In some ways, it's the biggest sporting event of the last decade. It's new and exciting for the United States."

In 2001, the first professional women's team in America debuted, the Women's United Soccer Association. Soccer was the last sport to launch a woman's professional team, but WUSA quickly made up for it with a string of successes. They took their players from the National Team and from top college draft talent. Attendance at their games surpassed expectations.

In 2004, the U.S. women's team once again won the gold! This was the last game for many of the veteran players who had won in the 1991 World Cup, and it was a great way to end their fantastic careers.

Although women's soccer in America developed later than in other countries, it has flourished, thanks to girls like Elisabeth Shue who loved the game and insisted on playing it and to smart, courageous women like Congresswomen Patsy Mink and Edith Green, who took legal steps to make sure they would be allowed to play.

About the Writers

Lisa Marie Peterson is also a writer and producer of *Law and Order: Special Victims Unit* and the writer of the TV series *In the House*. **Karen Janszen** is the screenwriter of many other movies, including *A Walk to Remember* and *Free Willy 2*.

Suzanne Weyn is a *New York Times* bestselling author with more than fifty titles to her credit. She has published books for children as young as kindergarten age, as well as novels for high school students. Suzanne's most recent novels include titles for young adults. *The Bar Code Tattoo* (2004) was selected by the American Library Association as a 2005 Quick Pick for Reluctant Young Adult Readers and is a 2007 Nevada Library nominee for Best Young Adult Fiction.